SHAPESHIFTER

HOLLY BENNETT

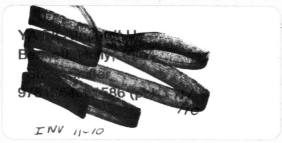
ORCA BOOK PUBLISHERS

Library and Archives Canada Cataloguing in Publication

Bennett, Holly, 1957-
Shapeshifter / written by Holly Bennett.

ISBN 978-1-55469-158-6

I. Title.

PS8603.E5595S53 2010   jC813'.6   C2009-907264-5

First published in the United States, 2010
Library of Congress Control Number: 2009942219

Summary: In order to escape the sorcerer who wants to control her gift of song, Sive must transform herself into a deer, leave the Otherworld and find refuge in Eire, the land of mortals.

 Mixed Sources
Cert no. SW-COC-001271
© 1996 FSC
FSC

Orca Book Publishers is dedicated to preserving the environment and has printed this book on paper certified by the Forest Stewardship Council.

Orca Book Publishers gratefully acknowledges the support for its publishing programs provided by the following agencies: the Government of Canada through the Canada Book Fund and the Canada Council for the Arts, and the Province of British Columbia through the BC Arts Council and the Book Publishing Tax Credit.

Cover artwork by Juliana Kolesova
Cover design by Teresa Bubela
Text design and typesetting by Nadja Penaluna
Author photo by Mark Peter Drolet

ORCA BOOK PUBLISHERS
PO Box 5626, STN. B
VICTORIA, BC CANADA
V8R 6S4

ORCA BOOK PUBLISHERS
PO Box 468
CUSTER, WA USA
98240-0468

www.orcabook.com
Printed and bound in Canada.
Printed on 100% PCW recycled paper.
13 12 11 10 • 4 3 2 1

To my mom, who taught me that diving into a good book is one of life's great pleasures.

CONTENTS

PREFACE

Those of you who have read *The Warrior's Daughter*
will already know about my love affair with Irish
mythology. But for the newcomers among you, here's a bit
of background:

Two thousand years ago, Ireland was inhabited by
the Iron-Age Celts. Much of what we know of their lives
and beliefs comes to us through the wonderful stories that
somehow survived in oral form through many, many genera-
tions until finally they were written down by early Christian
monks (who were supposed to be copying out the Bible).

Full of adventure, tragedy, magic and raw human
emotion, these stories seem to me just begging to be brought
alive for a modern audience. But since I am so often drawn to
the secondary characters—the ones you don't hear so much
about—rather than the heroes, and since I love making up
stories rather than just retelling them, my approach has been
to imagine an "untold tale" that lies behind the legend.

Shapeshifter is the story of Sive, a young woman from a
magical realm who was the hero Finn mac Cumhail's first
wife. At first I thought it was a story about fear and lost
love. But as I got to know Sive better, I realized that it is
really a story about courage, and about love's transformative
power. Like any good character, there is more to her than
first meets the eye.

For curious readers, I have included a version of the
ancient legend of Sive on page 242.

The year Sive became a woman, two things happened that would shape the course of her life:

She found her animal form.

And the dark druid, Far Doirche, fixed his eye upon her.

PART I
SIVE

ONE

She woke in the early dawn, the light still only a promise in the dissolving darkness. The woods called to her.

Sive had never been an early riser. In the otherworld land of Tir na nOg, there is no need to cut short the sweet ease of sleep. But this summer, the hush before sunrise filled her with expectancy. She loved to watch the world wake up, to see the leaves glow golden in the sun's first rays. She left her warm bed, slipped out of the sleeping house and took the path to the forest.

By the time the sun spilled its bright warmth over the world, she was sitting in her favorite spot, a fallen log coated with moss as soft and deep as her mother's silk cushions. It rested at the edge of a dark spring-fed pool. Soon, when the sun was higher and the breeze came up, the pool's surface would dance with ripples and light. Now it lay still and smooth as polished copper. Many animals and birds came to drink at the pool, but Sive was no longer elated when they appeared, or disappointed when they did not. She was content just to sit and watch the water and breathe the fragrant air.

SHE HAD ROAMED THESE woods for years, ever since she had first told her father about the longing in her heart. To take on the form of a creature wholly different, to be utterly changed and yet yourself—this, she thought, was a true marvel.

"How is it done?" she had asked, and then added in an eager rush, "And don't be saying I'm too young to understand. I've lost my first two milk teeth, and that means I'm no longer a baby." Triumphantly, she pulled down her bottom lip as proof.

Derg peered at the pink, gummy gap and nodded solemnly. "So you have, indeed. Then I will tell you the truth: you won't find your shape until you grow up, Sive. But that doesn't mean you can't do the work that comes before."

"What work is that?"

"You must spend time in the fields and the forests, with the creatures there. Watch them, listen to them. Learn to understand them."

As he talked, Derg pulled his young daughter onto his knee and played with the copper-gold waves that already reached halfway down her back.

"To become an animal, you must have a sense of kinship with the wild creatures," he explained. "Shapeshifting begins with the ability to place your heart and mind within an animal's skin. Only then will the skin itself take shape."

Sive pondered this and then squirmed around to face her father. Her lovely face was intent.

"How do you choose which animal to become?"

Her father laughed.

"You don't, daughter. Most of us have but one animal form; we become the animal most like our inner spirit. It's true that the greatest shapeshifters can take on the form of several beasts, but always there is something about each animal that speaks to the essence of the person. We cannot become what is foreign to our nature."

"What is your animal, then?"

Derg hesitated. Derg Dianscothach—Derg of the Quick Speech—was not a man of great power or ancestry, but his keen eye, quick understanding and artful tongue had earned him a place as the king's counselor, messenger and, sometimes, spy. It would not do for his animal form to become common knowledge.

"It is secret," he said finally. "Can I rely on you to keep it safe?" And with Sive's solemn nod, he bent and whispered into her ear.

AT FIRST HER FATHER went with her to the woods. He taught her how to mark her path to keep from losing

3

her way and which boggy, dangerous places to avoid. When he was convinced Sive could wander safely, he gave her leave to go alone—despite her mother's objections. But it did not take her long to notice the magpie that flitted from tree to tree, seemingly paying no mind but never far from sight. She complained about the way Derg watched over her, but she felt safer for it too.

She was so tense and eager on those first excursions that her very presence frightened the beasts away. She would strain her eyes and ears and nearly tremble with alertness and rarely saw more than a tomtit. Any unsuspecting deer or otter that did come into view would bolt the second it noticed her presence. "Be easy, Sive," her father would advise. "Be one of them. You would not get all excited if your sister walked into the room."

Perhaps not, she thought. But I would not be easy either.

Sive's half-sister Daireann was not the pleasant companion Derg saw. He thought it was kindness that prompted the young woman, on her rare visits from her father's home, to take the time to play and talk with a little girl. But Daireann was a subtle tormentor, one with a need to feel grand by making others—even children—feel small. Sive had learned to be on her guard, to wait for her sister's honeyed sting.

There was a game they played. "If I were an animal, what would I be?" Daireann would ask, and Sive would try to think of something clever and beautiful for her sister: a fox, a champion's horse, a falcon. But although her sister preened at the flattery, it did not soften her tongue.

"Daireann says I will be a rabbit," Sive told her father now. "Or a mouse."

"Does she indeed?" Derg considered this apparent insult.

"Perhaps she says this because you are quiet and small." He smiled at his daughter and shook his head. "But I believe she is wrong. You do have a gentle nature, something timid, perhaps, at times. But you are also strong and beautiful. Courageous too, at need."

Sive glowed at his words. She had known better than to argue with Daireann, but she knew her father was right. She knew, too, what animal called to her above all others.

If it were given to her to change shape, she would become a deer.

ON THAT STILL MORNING, Sive was alone. Her father had not flown with her since the winter, for Sive's mooncycles had begun and Derg knew her first change would not be far behind. That was a thing requiring solitude and not for another's eyes to witness.

She was not even thinking of shapeshifting. She simply rested in the peaceful stillness that many hours in the woods had taught her. It was this peace, she had learned, that allowed the creatures about her to relax in her presence and go about their business right under her nose. She let the swell of early birdsong fill her, let her eyes be lulled by the gentle motion of the leaves floating on the pool.

The underbrush trembled, and a red doe stepped into the clearing. She froze, lifting her black nose to check Sive's scent. Sive remained still, feeling the doe's caution and her curiosity, feeling her thirst. After a long moment, the deer picked her way down the muddy slope to the pool. And then—Sive could not keep her heart from tripping faster in a rush of delight—a young fawn, dappled with its white baby spots, came after its mam. All spindly legs and wide brown eyes, he braced himself on the bank beside his mother and lowered his muzzle to the water, whiffling uncertainly at its cold touch.

It was a moment of pure magic, watching that fawn learn to drink. Sive was filled with joy, as though it were her own baby's clever trick, as he stopped trying to suckle at the pool and instead lapped slowly with his tongue.

The fawn looked up from his drink, water streaming from his muzzle, and noticed Sive for the first time. It was comical how he started and stared. His mam startled, too, at his movement, and Sive thought they would both fly off, but after a quick check of the wind, the doe went back to her drink. Reassured, the fawn gazed at the girl and then with a friendly little tail flick began to skirt the pond toward her. He was unafraid, as though ambling over to meet one of his mam's herd mates. Sive was enchanted and then suddenly alarmed.

If a fawn so young became familiar with her shape

and scent, he might lose the fear of men that was his only defense against the hunters and their dogs. She saw him, confused and frightened, surrounded by the snarling hounds, and her heart twisted. It was her baby, her own, crying out as the sharp teeth sank into his neck.

Before she could jump to her feet and scare him off, before her intention to do so had fully formed, the change took her. The world rippled and blurred in her vision. Her body was lost to her in such an utterly strange gust of streaming sensation, blood and bone and flesh all swept into hurtling flux, that she could not think of it as her own. She was formless, and then she was sucked into the alien shape like molten metal flowing into a mould.

The fawn hesitated, one tiny hoof raised, as the stranger seemed to waver and grow dim. Then the figure came clear, and he could both smell and see her properly: a nearly grown fawn, a doe. He bucked a bit, playfully, and frisked over to her side.

Sive Remembers

I didn't dare move, my four legs as uncertain and untried as a newborn's. I thought my eyes had been injured in the change, for I had never dreamed the world could look so different. The lush, deep greens were gone, replaced by a yellow-brown wash that tinted everything—grass, leaves, tree trunks, even the other deer—shades of the same dun hue. Only later did I notice how brilliantly blue the sky blazed overhead and how clearly I could see into the shadowed places even in the dimmest twilight.

The triumph of what I had done thrilled through my blood, and the terror of it too. It had happened without my effort or will. What if I could not change back? Panic rose up in my breast, and I might have tried to claw my way out of my new skin if not for the fawn. He nuzzled beside me, nosing my flank as though checking for milk and then backing up awkwardly to find and lick my muzzle. The wonder of it pushed away the fear, and once I stopped being afraid, I understood that returning to my own form would be as simple as willing it.

I looked again through my new eyes, recognizing anew each familiar feature of the clearing. I stayed there all morning—so much to learn, there was. The air a complex stew of smells I didn't understand, far-off sounds so sharp and clear it seemed every moving thing in the forest was right beside me. The strangeness of losing my upright view, of a body stretched out parallel to the earth. So many legs! I thought they would tangle and trip me, but once I dared take a step with one hoof, the rest followed and I could soon walk easily around the pool.

When the sun was straight overhead—a time when all real deer rest hidden in their secret beds—I ventured away from the pool to explore the forest. I leapt over logs, I drifted silently through dark spruce groves, and when at last I came to a long bare slope, I ran. The swiftness, the power—it does not seem such a marvel to me now. But on that first day, flying could not have been more thrilling. It is a memory I cherish still, despite all that followed.

TWO

Wondrous though it seemed, shapeshifting was a minor magic compared to the power Sive's mother, Grian, had passed on to her. It was clear almost from the time Sive could lisp out a tune that she had the gift of song. The court women would call her over to their crying babies, and she would murmur a silly singsong child's lullaby, and they would first fall silent and then fall asleep. By the time Sive had ten summers, Grian was teaching her a proper repertoire, and after a battle or raid they would go together to sing to the wounded warriors, replacing their pain and anguish with the sweet mercy of sleep while the healers worked their magic and made them whole again.

Grian was not always the most attentive of mothers, but she trained her daughter carefully in the ways of the gift— to modulate her voice to bring weeping or giddy laughter or bright shining love to a listener, and then to ease it back so an audience could be entertained or soothed or moved without being overcome. And always, she and Derg both drilled into the girl the responsibility that comes with such power.

"It is no light trick to overwhelm a person's soul," said Grian. "Be sure you do it for right reasons, for there is no taking back what is done."

SIVE HAD OFTEN JOINED her mother for a song or two at a feast or gathering before being shooed away to bed. And she had given whole concerts for audiences of children and waiting women, even for small groups of nobles from her own sidhe. But now she was a woman, and she was about to give her first performance for the king himself and for his feast guests.

Of course she was nervous. The guests were looking for art, not magic, and though Sive knew she could not fail to stir their emotions, they would still see well enough if the music was faulty. Grian had rehearsed her endlessly, until their voices in duet seemed to pour from one mouth, and Sive's solo pieces were burnished to a high sheen.

"One last review?" her mother pressed, on the afternoon of the feast. And Sive, who had been dutiful and uncomplaining through long days of practice, dug in her heels and shook her head.

"No more, Ma. If I do not know them now, I never will. I am going for a walk to settle myself." Grian was high-strung and flighty of mind, all the more before a performance. At this moment, her very presence scraped on Sive's nerves.

Grian pressed her lips together, unhappy to see her daughter leave the house. "Be back in good time," she called. Sive couldn't blame her for being worried. She had a long-standing habit of disappearing into the woods.

THE LIVELY CROWD, the illustrious guests, the poets and harpists—none of them could lure Sive's mind from the singing to come. Not even the ambitious young warriors showing off their feats and tricks in the courtyard captured her interest for long. It was her first big test, and she was intent on proving herself worthy to sing alongside her mother. The crowd's warm response was a good sign, but only when Grian had smiled her relieved approval and whispered "Well done!" in her daughter's ear, could Sive relax and join in the gathering.

With the entertainment done, the food and drink came out in earnest. When the stars were bright in the night sky, the nobles would sit down to the king's high feast. But until then, the great side tables that lined the hall were heaped with a changing array of meats and dainties, enough to appease the mightiest appetite.

Sive wandered about the room, sampling dishes and stealing sidelong glances at the guests. Several times she was stopped and complimented on her singing. It made her flush with pride and pleasure, and though she did her best to give a gracious reply, she knew her inexperience showed. She caught sight of her father at the king's side, making introductions and helping the conversation flow easily, and had the childish wish he would do so for her instead. There were many strange faces in the hall and among them more than one man she would not mind meeting.

She was glad Daireann had not made the journey to attend. Her half-sister would be sure to find a way to mar Sive's evening. "Watch you don't strain your precious voice," Daireann had cooed at her one day when Sive was careless enough to react angrily to one of her digs—and for the first time, Sive realized that Daireann was jealous. Daireann had the powerful father, the luxurious court, the prestige that comes with a great name—yet she did not have what Sive had. Though the great Bodb Dearg, Grian's first husband and Daireann's father, was the master of all music, their daughter had a pretty voice, no more.

WHEN SHE FIRST SAW Far Doirche, it was not the handsome green-eyed sorcerer who caught her attention, but the ragged boy who trailed at his heel.

Sive had never before seen a person starved for food. Among her people, whom mortals called the People of the Sidhe, there was plenty for the taking. To be sure there were those who were powerful and high, and others who served, but since there was no end of food and warmth and fine things, there was no need for any to be without. Or so she thought.

This boy, though: he was only a little younger than Sive herself, on the edge of his change to manhood, yet still smooth-cheeked and slight. Skinny, rather, with bony shoulders hunched under a tunic so worn and patched she could not fathom how his master would allow such a thing to appear at a grand gathering. He glanced at the nearest food table, the longing plain on his face. Such a gaunt, pale face it was, with dark hollows under his eyes, as if he had not slept for days. Then his master moved on, and the boy jerked his gaze away and scrambled after.

Sive looked then to the man he served. His dress was impeccable, all bright silks and fine linen. Glossy honey-brown hair hung smooth down his back. He made his way through the crowd, exchanging greetings and cordial talk, and the eyes of his acquaintances never strayed to the boy at his heel. It was as though he did not exist.

The sweetness of her victory vanished in a gust of hot anger. It was shameful, a guest to be treated so. No one would go hungry, not at her sidhe.

She grabbed a bowl and, passing over the delicate sweets and morsels, ladled in a generous serving of stew. She floated a couple of biscuits on top, took a goblet of mead in her other hand and went straight to the boy.

Startled dark eyes lifted to meet hers when she spoke.

"Sir, I see you have not yet eaten. Will you not enjoy the hospitality of the king of Sidhe Ochta Cleitigh? Or perhaps our food does not please you?" She held out the bowl. "I am Sive, daughter of Derg, who is counselor to King Fiachna."

He eyed the stew, then glanced quickly up at his master. Far Doirche was deep in conversation with two other men. Thin fingers crept slowly toward the bowl.

"My thanks to you," he whispered.

Sive could not help but stare as he spooned it in. She had never seen a person eat like that, furtive and hurried at the same time. Like a hound at a sheep carcass, she thought.

He had almost finished when Far Doirche spoke his name.

"Oran."

His voice was low and musical, pleasant to hear. Yet Oran flinched as though he had been struck. He thrust the bowl into Sive's hands and wheeled to bow his head to Far.

"Please forgive me, master." The words were barely audible.

She could not leave it alone. There was something so wrong here. For the first time, she spoke directly to Far Doirche.

"Surely there is no need for a servant to apologize for eating from the common table? The food is here for all to enjoy. I offered it, so if there is any wrong done, it is mine."

He did not look angry. His face, like his voice, was pleasant. A bystander would have said his stare was simply curious, or perhaps admiring. But those green eyes weighed on Sive, drilled into her, and she was suddenly, unreasonably, afraid.

"You are the singer," he observed, his manner courtly and gentle. "A wonderful voice."

"Thank you, sir," she managed. A cold breath flowed over her ankles—surely just a draft of winter air dancing through the hall after the heavy doors had been opened, but it seemed to come from *him*. His eyes had not shifted from her face.

"Oran's job is to attend me. He will have a time to eat." He smiled gently. "Of course, to refuse a lovely girl's generosity would be impolite."

Far's gaze finally shifted away to rest on the boy. "Have you finished with the stew?"

Oran's nod was almost imperceptible. "Yes, master."

"Good. Then why don't you take the mead with you, and we'll continue."

They left her then and made their way down the crowded hall. But she noticed that Oran left his mead goblet on the first table they passed.

Oran Remembers

How is it that people did not shudder at first sight of him, go cold with gooseflesh or faint with premonition? But I have seen it so often—it is only to those who know what he is that the evil is so plainly in view.

And what of it, if she did not understand the risk she took with her kindness to me? It was long since anyone had paid me any mind at all. Sive placed herself between me and the Dark Man's displeasure. I will never forget that.

But I will always regret it. For he marked her that day, marked her as surely as he turned the mead in my goblet to mud. Every person on his path he sorts into one of two categories: those who are of no use to him, and those he may turn to his own ends. Sive had unwittingly caught his eye. And now he bent his mind upon her, and I could only pray that he would find no hold there for his dark dreams.

THERE WAS LITTLE TIME to dwell on Oran, or on his strange master, for Sive was soon overtaken by her mother. Grian was in her element, bright-eyed and with a high color to her cheeks. Sometimes a flush like that spoke of temper, but not tonight. Grian was happiest in a crowd, whether singing for them or bantering and laughing in the midst of a circle of men. She thrived on attention, and Derg, it seemed, was wise enough not to take offence when she fluttered her lashes and arched her neck for an admiring man. Perhaps, mused Sive, his patience, along with his unending devotion, was how her father was able to keep Grian's love when Bobd Dearg had not.

But Grian had not forgotten she had a young daughter just recently come to womanhood. "How are you managing? Enjoying yourself? Who have you spoken to?"

The questions came in a stream, with no space for a reply. Sive did not attempt one but only smiled and nodded. She did feel awkward in her new role, unpracticed at the gracious talk her parents excelled at, but she *was* enjoying herself.

How not? She had sung well, the pale green silk of her gown flowed over her slender form in a lustrous wave, and she had seen more than one head turn to watch her pass. On this night Sive stood on the very brink of her adult life, full of promise.

Grian fussed at Sive's hair, tucking stray tendrils around her ears and then gathering up the weight of it from her back and shaking it gently into place. Looping her arm through her daughter's, she began strolling through the hall, her mouth close to Sive's ear.

"Men have been asking after you," she murmured. Sive's heart sped up, with pleasure and with alarm too. Would her parents betroth her this very night? Surely not, and she so young? Grian nodded, a subtle, tiny dip, toward a man to their right. "Him, for instance." Sive had a brief glimpse of a broad back, dark hair, a cloak of many rich colors. "That is Irial, of Sidhe Finnachaidh. A man of fine reputation."

"Who else?" Sive sounded a bit breathless, her voice betraying her.

"Oh, several." Grian gave a brief, silvery laugh. "I have hardly ever had to rebuff so many in one night."

Sive stopped. "What do you mean, rebuff?" Fear that her mother would entertain these men's inquiries was replaced with indignation that she had not.

"I told them you were but a bud half-blossomed, as they could very well see for themselves, and that they must wait for the full flowering before buzzing about you like bees."

Her tart words made her daughter stiffen. Does she mock me? Sive wondered. The thought came, mean and angry, that Grian only wanted to keep these men buzzing about herself.

But Grian's manner softened as she felt Sive's reaction.

"Ah, now, daughter." She glanced about the crowded hall and coaxed Sive into a quieter alcove. She touched her face softly, found Sive's eyes with her own, and Sive felt her sulkiness waver.

"There is no need to be rushing after men, dear one. It's long ages you will have, for lovers and husbands too." She nudged Sive and smirked. "Maybe even both in the same body, if you are lucky."

Sive stared at her, startled, and then dissolved into giggles. She was old enough at least to share a woman's joke, her mother was telling her. Her injured pride was healed.

The horns interrupted them, calling the nobles to feast. Grian, Sive saw, had already left their conversation, her mind flitting ahead eagerly to the next event. Sive smiled ruefully. Her mother could be kind, even wise, but unless music was involved, you couldn't hold her focus for long.

Grian tugged at Sive's arm. "Come and eat, then," she said. "We will be well placed to admire the view."

Derg was not overly highborn, but he had the ear of the king. That, and the marriage he had made to Grian, gave his family a good place in the feasting hall. Sive followed her mother into the hall. Always a handsome room, it had been transformed into a wonder of light and color. Sive lingered to admire the living garlands twining up each column, coaxed into lavish bloom despite the snow outside.

A shiver, as if someone had dropped a little handful of that snow down the back of her neck, crawled up her spine. She looked around and then quickly dropped her gaze. That man, the one with the ragged servant, was entering the feasting hall. Sive hurried after Grian before he could draw near. She hoped his seat would be far away from hers.

THREE

T he seasons danced through their cycle. How many times, Sive could not say, for time held little meaning in the undying lands. Surely several winters went by, time enough for her to understand the wisdom of her mother's words. She had indeed been a half-opened bud, but now she came fully into her woman's form. The childish roundness in her cheeks melted away, and she found the grace in her limbs. She learned, too, to be at ease in a crowd and to converse with a stranger, to accept a compliment with calm pleasure and then turn the talk back to the speaker so that it flowed between them. She was a young woman near the height of her beauty, only a few seasons away from the appearance she would keep to the end of time.

She was asked to sing often, growing confident in her art. Sive and her mother were sometimes invited to one or other of the neighboring sidhes, and though Grian filled her ear with the usual mother's cautions, she did not hinder Sive from meeting the men who asked after her. Sive was confused, and even troubled, by the uncharacteristic caution shown by some of these men. It took her a while to realize that her gift was the cause: they were both fascinated and frightened by it, as if at any moment she might open her mouth and plunge them into helpless, unwilling love. Because it had never occurred to her to misuse her voice, their fears seemed foolish. Yet the power was real. She could, if she wished, sing a king and his servants to sleep and rob him of his treasures, take revenge on a rival by plunging her into despairing grief, or, yes, compel a man to love her. But that was not the sort of love Sive wanted.

She did not go to the woods as often as before. Right after her first change it had been all she wanted to do. She had practiced until she could transform effortlessly, her body streaming into deer form with a mere thought. As a deer, she learned the forest in a whole new way, through different paths and different senses. It was a constant fascination, with a hint of danger to add an edge of excitement. For although Sive was swifter than any real deer, and smarter, there is no wild creature whose safety from those who hunt her is assured.

But her life was changing. She was busy creating her outward face, learning to be a woman in the world. Shapeshifting no longer seemed so wondrous but only an amusement better suited to a younger self.

"YOUR PARDON, LADY. Your mother is asking after you." Sive put down her embroidery and followed Grian's maidservant.

Grian sat in the bright gazebo, open to the air and sunshine, that Derg had built for her to enjoy in fine weather. A slender man, bearing the flagged spear of a messenger, stood by her side.

"Sit down, daughter. There is great news." Sive sat in silence, keeping to herself the thought that her mother looked more troubled than pleased.

Grian waved in the vague direction of the messenger. "An invitation to sing—from Bodb Dearg himself! He is hosting a council of all the men of his western realm. He has heard of your talent and wishes to hear your voice."

"Only me?" Sive had never traveled to Bodb's great dwelling on the shores of Loch Dearg, even with her family.

Her mother's smile was fleeting—impossible to tell if there was bitterness there, or amusement. "Of course only you. I am not so foolish as to insult a man like Bodb and then return to rub his nose in it." Her voice became brisk. "It is a great opportunity for you, Sive. And it is certain you will not be alone. Daireann will see to you."

"Daireann. Of course." Sive kept her thoughts about her half-sister to herself as well.

"You must leave in two days' time," Grian announced. "This man will stay and escort you there. Nessa, see him settled now." And with that the maidservant led the messenger into the house, and the two women were alone.

Sive's mind was full of questions, but the one that pushed its way forward surprised her.

"Why did you leave Bodb?" She had asked this once before, as a young girl, and Grian's sharp reply had made it clear it was her mother's own business and no one else's.

Today, though, Grian sighed and shrugged. "I suppose you should know, if you are after going there."

She regarded her daughter for a long moment.

"I was young, only a little past your own age, when Bodb asked for me. And the prospect of such a grand match went to my head, I suppose, for my father had little work to persuade me to go to him." Grian's father, Manannan, had an ancient and mighty name himself; he was, in fact, the one who had created the enchanted barriers that hid their lands from the mortal men of Gael. Sive could well imagine that he favored the match.

"I was not his first wife, nor his last," Grian continued. "But it was lovely at first. We made music together nearly every day, and he came often to my bed. I was his new young bride, and he craved my company."

Sive began to see the end of the story, even before her mother confirmed it. "But a great man has great demands on him, I suppose, and it must be said I am something demanding myself. His ardor cooled, and even more his interest, and he turned back to the running of his many households and his hunting and his music, and I was left alone. And later, when your sister was but half-grown, he brought home another wife, a beauty with hardly a brain in her head."

Grian shrugged. "I bore it long enough. It was a rich and pleasant life that I had, but I was not happy in it. And then came the year we held the great gathering of all the sidhes. I sang, of course, and Derg was one of many who came to praise the music. But he was different from the others. Many men are full of fine talk, but it's rare to find one who listens just as well. When we talked, he would listen as though there were no other sound in the world. And that was only a part of all I loved about him. When he asked me to return here with him, I didn't even let myself think it through. I just said yes."

"Have you ever regretted it?"

A long silence, so long Sive thought she had overstepped and would get no reply. Then Grian smiled. "At times. I have come down in the world, there is no doubt of that. But what I return to is this: he still puts me at the center of his heart. He has no desire for a collection of women, but only for me. I like that."

Sive nodded. Any woman would like that, she supposed, but especially her mother. She rose from her chair—there was a journey to organize—but Grian waved her back.

"Stay a moment. There is one more thing."

Grian leaned forward, her eyes intent. "Sive, when I left Bodb I was already pregnant, though I didn't yet know it. It is possible you are his child, not Derg's." Startled, Sive sank back into her chair.

"It is in my mind that Bodb has asked for you to see what manner of woman you have become, perhaps even to consider claiming you as his own." She raised a hand against Sive's vehement headshake. "It is nothing against Derg as a father. He has been good to you, as I well know. But it would be to your advantage, Sive. If he offers it, you should accept Bodb's protection."

Now Sive did rise, flustered and confused. "If he wanted to acknowledge me, he could have done so long since," she said.

"All the same. If he claims you, don't respond in haste, is all I am saying."

Sive didn't want to think about her mother's words, much less discuss them. "I'll pack now," she said, as she rose and fled to the house.

FOUR

odb's crystal house dazzled in the sunshine, brighter than the glittering surface of the great lake below it. Sive took a deep breath, marvelling at the colors of sky, hills and water reflected from its walls. Now she understood what her mother had meant by "coming down in the world." She had thought their own king's palace very beautiful, but this was beyond anything in her experience. Grian had been right, she saw now, to talk the king into providing a full retinue of maidens and guards for the journey. Sive was not sure what she would do with so many servants, but at least she would make an adequate entrance on behalf of their sidhe.

She was led through rich, airy rooms and delicate gardens to Bodb himself. He was a handsome, commanding man with thick golden hair pulled into a knot at the back of his head. He was not, as Sive had imagined, lounging at his ease, fingering his famous harp; rather he strode briskly into the room with the air of a man with a long list of tasks to see to—which of course he was, with guests arriving from all corners of his kingdom. He gave Sive a gracious but brief welcome, thanking her for coming, introducing her to the master of revels, and pointedly *not* asking after her mother.

Not exactly a greeting for a long-lost child, she noted wryly. Grian, it seemed likely, had been mistaken with that fond theory.

"Daireann is looking forward to seeing you," Bodb offered. He frowned. "I had thought she would be here to greet you. She insisted you share her rooms, so that you will feel more at home."

Of course she did, thought Sive as she mustered what she hoped was a grateful smile. It was hard to imagine this lovely palace held a single uncomfortable corner, but Sive had a feeling Daireann would find it.

"I'VE PUT YOU OVER HERE, so you'll have more privacy." Daireann motioned to the corner of her sitting room, a spacious, bright chamber joined to a smaller sleeping room by a wide, arched opening, both so draped and swathed with gaudy silks that Sive felt swaddled in a peacock's breast. "There's a settle already there, so we won't need to clutter up the room with an extra pallet."

Sive eyed the narrow bench warily. Elaborately carved, heaped with overstuffed cushions and raised at the head,

it would be delightful for lazing away a dull afternoon—
and a nightmare to sleep on.

"Of course there's no room for your women in here, or
with my maids." Daireann motioned vaguely to the door
beyond her bedstead, which presumably led to a third room
housing her servants. "With so many people staying, we've
had to put all but the most important guests' attendants
in the outbuildings. But I expect you're used to seeing to
yourself."

It was masterful how she did it, wrapping so many
slights in a single pronouncement. Sive's growing anger—
there was ample room for one companion to stay with her,
and she was willing to bet she was the only female guest in
the place sleeping without one—was almost overshadowed
by grudging admiration. She forced a bright smile.

"It's lovely, Daireann," she said. "You're very generous to
share your chambers with me."

"It's the least a sister can do." Daireann drifted into her
sleeping room and admired herself before the tall mirror
mounted beside her bed. She arched her neck, tossed
back her yellow hair and slipped another bracelet up her
white arm. Sive waited, knowing there was more to come.
Daireann never left a gracious phrase unbarbed. "In any
case, I don't suppose we shall see much of each other. There
are several men courting me, and you'll be busy with the
other workers."

With a sisterly smile as venomous as a poisoned arrow,
Daireann excused herself and bustled off, leaving Sive to

discover for herself where her women had been housed and when dinner might be expected.

HE HAD A TUMBLE of dark curls and black eyes that flashed when he smiled, and he was sitting to Sive's left at the next morning's meeting called to organize the performers. Somehow her attention kept drifting toward him rather than the master of revels, an earnest fellow with a droning voice. The schedule was not taxing: over the five-day gathering, performers were asked to share their art at every other dinner and at two midday meals. "You all are our esteemed guests," gushed the revelmaster. "If there is any comfort or hospitality lacking to you, you have only to let me know."

A proper bed would be a start, thought Sive. After a night spent bobbing in a sea of cushions, she was less than rested. Her women had fared better, sharing one room but each with a freshly stuffed pallet, clean bedclothes and a rack to hang out her gowns.

During the introductions that followed, Sive discovered she was the only female singer—there was a pair of sisters who played flute and harp, and two male singers—and the only artist not from the west. The young man who had caught her eye was Elatha, a poet from a sidhe on the ocean's edge, in the rocky, wild country that thrust out like fingers from the southwest corner of the Island. As they were leaving, Sive managed to put herself in the arched doorway at the same time as him.

"You've come a long way," he said.

"Aye," she agreed. "And so have you, to be sure."

"Yet my sidhe is within Bodb's realm, while yours is not. Not to malign your talents, which I am sure are marvellous, but I wonder what led our king to invite you."

She glanced up, looking for a slight, but the dark eyes showed only friendly curiosity.

"Ah, well. There's a family connection."

Elatha pointed to the right, where several of the artists were ambling through a small door that led outdoors. Bright sunshine spilled onto the flagstones each time it opened.

"There is a delightful garden out there. Shall we take a look, and you can tell me more about your family ties?"

Elatha held out his arm, and Sive took it.

It was a perfect golden autumn day, and the garden was a sprawling delight. Sunny banks of flowers, herbs and fruit trees gradually gave way to cool shaded pathways. At last they emerged onto a long strand edging the lake. Someone had thoughtfully provided benches to rest on.

"I would love to live by the water," Sive said. "I am drawn to it like a salmon."

"This is not water, but only a mucky pond," Elatha teased. "You should live where I do. There is water everywhere."

"I have hardly ever seen the ocean," Sive confessed.

"How can that be?" He feigned astonishment. "Have you no ocean in the east?"

"Only on the coast, where I, sadly, do not live."

"Yes, and speaking of where you live"—Elatha gave Sive a little nudge with his elbow—"what are these connections of yours?"

"Do you know Daireann?"

"Oh yes." Did she imagine it, or were his eyes suddenly guarded? "Everybody knows Daireann."

"I am her half-sister. We have the same mother."

There was no mistaking it. Subtly, but definitely, Elatha straightened up so that the space between them became politely formal. "You are Daireann's sister?"

"*Half*-sister," she corrected. And then, throwing both caution and etiquette to the winds, she said, "Don't worry, I am nothing like her!"

Elatha burst into surprised laughter. He was really very lovely when he laughed, white teeth gleaming and curls blowing in the wind.

"Is that a promise?" he asked.

"Yes, but…do you have something against her?"

"Oh…" He sighed. "One of my brothers had a bit of a romance with her once. Perhaps it's enough to say it went badly and ended worse."

"It is," Sive agreed. "And for my part, perhaps it's enough to say she's making me sleep on a heap of cushions when there are beds aplenty."

Another chuckle. Black eyes dancing with mischief. "Ah, now. I thought you looked something on the tired side at our little meeting, and the revels not yet begun!"

SIVE GAVE HER FIRST performance that night, and when she was done there were many wanting to meet her. Still it was Elatha she looked for, the color rising to her cheeks when she saw him in the crowd, her heart tripping into a glad canter when he made his way over to her. He was full of gentle teasing and merry laughter, and when the night's official pleasures came to an end, she was happy to join him once more on the moonlit paths of Bodb's garden.

She returned to her room late, braced for Daireann's scolding, but her half-sister was not there. Probably doing the same as myself, Sive thought. She did her best to pat her pillows into something resembling a mattress. With so many men to court, perhaps Daireann would be this late every night, and Sive's own romance would escape her notice.

THE NEXT MORNING, Daireann was not there, her bed unslept in. One of her women made a surprising offer.

"You might just as well sleep in her bed from now on, and leave that awful contraption," she said. "We'll not see my lady for a while yet."

"Why not?"

"Hasn't she set her sights on some son of the Gael? It's all we've heard for days. On and on about this Finn mac Cumhail and his mighty feats. She's off to the mortal world to woo him."

The woman bent over to gather up Daireann's gown, left in a heap on the floor. "I almost feel sorry for him, whoever he is," she offered. "They say mortal men can't resist our women."

"DO YOU KNOW much of the mortal world?" Sive asked Elatha that afternoon. He had just recited the Battle of Tailltin for Bodb's guests, telling of the final battle between the Gaels and the children of Danu. Sive had never really thought about the world they had lost or the people who had taken their place. The invaders must have been mighty warriors indeed, she supposed, hampered as they were with their frail lives and feeble magic skills, to have conquered her ancestors.

"A little," he said. "Is it a history lesson you're looking for? I'd have thought we'd done enough of that for now." And he picked up one of her shining plaits in both hands and ran his cheek down its coppery length. "This, now. This is a treasure to inspire poetry."

Sive dimpled at his words but kept hold of the thread of her thought.

"I was wondering if you had heard of a man named Finn mac Cumhail."

Elatha looked up from his explorations, his face bright with enthusiasm. "Finn? Of course. That is a man deserving of fame in any world."

The dark eyebrows drew together and he dropped her braid.

"What is your interest, exactly? If you're asking me to sing the praises of my rival, I won't do it!"

"My sister is after courting him." Sive had a momentary qualm—did Daireann intend to keep that a secret?—and shrugged it off. Family loyalty between her and Daireann was a weak bond at best.

Suspicion crinkled into amusement. "Ah. My best to him. Well then, what did you want to know?"

"Anything. I've never heard of him before now."

"Have you not? And he your neighbor! His dun is practically next door to you, on the Hill of Almhuin."

Sive shrugged, embarrassed to discover her own ignorance. She knew, of course, that the mortal world existed like a shadow of their own, and that there were places where the enchanted veil between them could be drawn back and passed through. But she had never done it, nor even wondered much about it. It gave her a funny feeling to think that the hills so familiar to her existed in another world, where an entirely different people built entirely different settlements.

"He leads the Fianna, a warrior troop that answers only to the High King of Eire," Elatha continued. "Mighty fighters to a man, they are. But Finn—he is different. The blood of our people runs in his veins, for one thing, for his mother, Muirne, is half-sister to Lugh of the Long Hand. And he is farseeing for a mortal; they say he has tasted the Nuts of Wisdom." Elatha laughed. "Perhaps the Nuts of Wisdom will gird him against your sister."

FIVE

The next two days passed in a whirl of feasting, music and the most delightful flirtation. Sive had never been courted so ardently and certainly not by a man so pleasing. Elatha, like her, had most of the day free while Bodb and his chieftains conducted their business, and he made it clear he wished to spend as much of it as possible at Sive's side. By the time evening fell and it was time for her to sing, she felt half-drunk with the heady wine of first love, and she knew her voice was more powerful and moving than ever before.

On the fourth day of Bodb's gathering, Sive sang at the midday meal. It was a smaller crowd, as Bodb had taken many of his guests hunting on the bare grassy mountains and deep valleys of his land. Elatha had been brought along to witness their feats and adventures and recount them that evening. "It is one of the duties of the poets, to sing the praises of their hosts and guests," Elatha had said resignedly. "But tomorrow is our day!" They had been delighted to learn they both had the last day of the gathering free and had planned a long ride into the countryside together.

As she had been taught, Sive swept her gaze around the room as she sang, including all the audience in her song. Many of the faces were familiar to her now, but it was a new face that caught her eyes in passing and held them fast. Though years had passed since their first meeting, Sive recognized him instantly.

Far Doirche. The searching, greedy way he stared at her made her voice catch and falter on its note. She was trapped in his green eyes, eyes bright and hard as emeralds, and the hair rose up on her neck as she realized she could not pull her gaze from his.

With rising panic, she struggled both to keep the song flowing from her lips and to free herself from Far's hold. When at last, with a gentle smile, he released her, it took all of her will not to run from the room. She finished her pieces, but it was a poor performance, for the confusion and fear would not leave her. How had he done that to her— and why?

A meal in the same room as him was more than she could face. Sive waved a quick thanks and hurried from the hall, heading straight for the refuge of her chamber.

"...IGNORANT, RUDE, dim-witted, coarse-tongued, ill-made..."

Sive had closed the chamber door before realizing that Daireann was back and in a full-blown temper. Her half-sister struggled out of her travel-stained clothing as she cursed, while three of her women stood by in cautious silence.

With a cry of anger Daireann balled up cloak and gown together and hurled them at the fireplace. Reaching for the clean gown one woman offered wordlessly, she registered Sive's presence at last and rounded on her.

"Who gave you leave—oh, it's you. Wonderful." She sighed, control returning by degree. "Take my advice, Sive. Don't believe those stories of the high deeds of mortal men. If I am just after meeting one of the best, they are all stupid and boorish beyond telling!" Two spots of color burned high on Daireann's cheeks as her anger threatened to flare up again.

Sive tried to gather her frayed wits as she edged over to the settle. Evidently Daireann had been unsuccessful in her pursuit.

The same woman who had offered Daireann's bed to Sive worked up her courage and spoke.

"But my lady, you are so beautiful. Surely he could not fail to be captivated. Is it possible he did not understand what you offered?"

Daireann was mollified enough by the flattery to answer. "He said he would stay by his men." She sniffed. "His precious Fianna. I told him he could bed down with them too, then, since they outweighed any woman in his heart."

37

A bitter smile curved her lips. "And then I put him under a spell to make him curse and insult his men so offensively that there will be no Fianna remaining for him to lead!"

She flounced her head, bringing Sive once again into her vision. Daireann's anger faded as she took a long, appraising look.

"What's the matter with you? You're pale as milk. Are you ill?"

Sive shook her head.

"What, then?"

Now Sive wished she had claimed illness, for Daireann would not rest until she pulled out the whole story. On the other hand, she might know something about Far Doirche.

"A man in the audience frightened me," she confessed. How childish that sounded.

Evidently Daireann thought so too, for she burst into tinkly laughter, her own troubles forgotten.

"Dear, dear, little sister. Are you not a bit old to be afraid of men?"

Sive could not summon a smile to meet the teasing. "Daireann, his name is Far Doirche, and when he looked at me, I could not pull my eyes away no matter how I tried. Do you know of him?"

"Far Doirche! He is here?" Daireann was serious now. "There are many who avoid him and those who speak against him, but that is because he is a druid of tremendous power. Of course there will be detractors and jealous resentments."

"But Daireann, what does he want with me?"

"You?" Sive's sister shrugged. "I doubt he wants anything. I expect he was merely amusing himself."

Daireann went into the adjoining room to stand before the long copper mirror, frowning before her image.

"Too dark," she said to her women. "I'll fade into the walls in this. Bring me the new red silk."

BY THE TIME BODB and his men came clattering and shouting back to the dun with a couple of deer and a boar strung onto poles and, from the sounds of them, a head start on the night's drinking, Sive had convinced herself that Daireann was right. Or perhaps Far Doirche remembered how she had fed his servant, and had held her that way to warn her against interfering again. Well, she would heed his warning, if that's what it was, and stay well out his way until it was time to return home.

Still, she wished she could see Elatha. He would be closeted away until nightfall, feverishly composing his lay, and Sive would have to be content with the memory of his kisses and sweet words. He had already promised to visit her soon in Sidhe Ochta Cleitigh. Perhaps then he would speak to her father about a match.

DAIREANN COMMANDEERED her for dinner, and for once Sive was glad of her sister's company. She did not want to risk finding herself seated beside the green-eyed druid.

When Elatha stood up to recite the day's adventures, the cheering was rowdy and boisterous, quite different from the quiet respect given to his histories and love tales. Sive felt the color flush into her cheeks just from the sight of him and hoped Daireann was not watching too closely. He looked a little nervous, she thought, and no wonder: this was not only an artistic challenge but also a politically sensitive exercise. His lay was masterful, though, giving all the most important guests their moment to shine and with a subtle emphasis on Bodb Dearg's prowess and generosity. He makes it sound like skewering a pig is a heroic feat, thought Sive. That was unfair, she supposed: wild boars really were dangerous, quite capable of killing a dog or a man. But her time as a deer had given her a new perspective on the hunt, and she could not help but think the boar's spirited defence against a host of armed enemies the more courageous.

It was as Elatha finished, and the cheers and yells of the hunting party erupted, that Sive knew something was wrong. Elatha bowed and smiled his thanks, but the smile was a pale ghost of his usual merry grin and it did not touch his black eyes. Those eyes, sweeping the crowd as he held up a hand in salute, skittered over the top of her head and would not meet her own. Moments later they did come to rest upon something—or someone—at the back of the room. Sive craned her neck, trying to follow his sightline.

Far Droiche stood in a shadowed alcove, a dim figure erratically lit by the flaring walltorches. Glittering eyes in a pale face. He gave a little nod in Elatha's direction, his expression unchanging.

Sive's body drained of warmth, cold seeping into her bones where no cloak or fire could reach it. She looked back at her lover, not caring now if Daireann noticed. He was leaving, making his way slowly but obviously through the crowd of loud, back-slapping men that had gathered to congratulate him. Leaving without speaking one word to her!

Never run after a man—at least not in public view. It was one of Grian's bits of motherly advice, but Sive turned a deaf ear. Elatha had already reached the door. She jumped up from her bench, ignoring Daireann's startled exclamation, and hurried after him.

"Stop, please! Elatha! Just for one moment!"

He was striding across Bodb's lawns with a speed that left no doubt he was trying to get away. He did not break stride or look around at Sive's pleas, nor at the sob of hurt and bewilderment that escaped her. But just as she slumped to a stop, he made the slightest gesture of his hand, almost too subtle to see: an index finger beckoning her on.

Secrecy. *He's asking for secrecy,* she realized, and she began walking again, slumped and slow as if she had given up, watching from under her eyebrows to see where he went.

Elatha made a turn behind an outbuilding and disappeared. How to follow, without following? Sive forced herself to walk in the opposite direction and think. If Elatha wanted her to meet him, he must be headed somewhere she could guess easily, but others would not.

He was waiting on the strand when she arrived. The lakeside had become a special place for them, but Elatha's face when he turned to her was not the face of an eager lover.

"You did not tell me you were promised to the Dark Man!"

"The—? I am not. I do not even know who this Dark Man is!"

"The sorcerer, Far Doirche. He says you are his intended."

The coldness was back now, cold that pimpled the skin on Sive's arms and made her neck prickle. But there was anger, too, bracing as the wind off the water that lifted her hair and pulled at her skirts.

"Well, he is not *my* intended. Nor has he made his *intention* known to any of my family!"

The flare of anger faded away as Sive saw Elatha's expression soften from accusation to sadness.

"Ah, dear heart. I should have known. He lied to me."

He will not fight for me. She saw it in the slump of his shoulders, the resignation in his voice. The fire of his eyes replaced with pity.

Elatha grabbed her arms, suddenly urgent.

"Sive, listen to me. If you do not want this match, you must leave. Don't wait until morning even. Just gather your people and go. Perhaps if you are not under his nose, his attention will fall elsewhere."

"But why? Why cannot I simply refuse him?" She remembered once again the pull of those green eyes, the threat behind them, and wondered just how possible it would be to refuse him anything. Elatha's impatient snort came like an answer.

"Do you think he is called the Dark Man in jest? He is a master of dark sorcery, Sive, and he does not hesitate to use it. Driven by his own will, he is, so hungry for power that no law or bond, not of friendship nor of blood, will temper his ambition. He has made it quite clear what will happen to me—and to you—if I am seen in your company again." He looked at her now, and she saw that she had guessed correctly. He would leave her to Far Doirche, though it hurt him to do it.

"Go away from him," he urged again. "I cannot help you, and for that I am sorry. But I swear by the earth and sky I would rather be dead in the grave than see you in his hands."

He glanced up and down the deserted beach, as if Far Doirche's eyes might even now be upon them. "We cannot risk speaking again. I will walk the strand and return by a different road. I wish you well, Sive." But the sorrow in his eyes told her he foresaw a different fate. She watched the tall shoulders move away from her, knowing it was for the last time.

"Elatha—wait!"

He turned, reluctantly.

"Why does he want *me*?"

"Do you not know?" Elatha raised his hands in a half-stifled gesture that seemed to Sive both angry and defeated. "You have a power he does not. The Dark Man wants your voice."

He turned again, and this time he kept walking until he disappeared from view.

SIX

*S*ive Remembers

Of course he did not forget. When the Dark Man sets his sights on a thing, there is no forgetting.

I could not bring myself to tell my parents what had happened. My mother accepted the easy explanation—that I was home early, and prone to tears, because of a failed love affair. She said only, in her practical way, "Don't take it too hard, love. The world is full of men. It doesn't do to bind yourself to the first one who comes down the path."

My father is a better listener, and he must have sensed there was more to my tale for he sought me out in private and gently gave me the chance to say more. But why worry him about something that might not come to pass?

So I thought. Now I wonder if those thoughts were truly my own, or if Far Doirche had somehow bound my tongue.

Autumn was blown away by a snowy winter, which melted into spring, and still he did not come. And I began first to hope, then to believe that I was safe from him. By the time the night air was nipped with the first hint of autumn frost, I hardly ever thought of him.

And then he came.

THE THREE FRIENDS ambled down the lane, their arms filled with the last autumn blooms, crowns of wound-wort and cranesbill circling their heads. They chatted and laughed as they walked, perpetually young, glowing with health, apparently free of care.

A tall man stepped into the road in front of them. He must have been standing behind a tree trunk or in the shadows of the shrubbery, for he seemed to appear out of the air. Two of the women started, their smiles of greeting guarded, but the third stood frozen, her flowers fallen heedless to the ground. Her hazel eyes were wide in a face drained of color.

"Hello, Sive." The man's smile was easy and disarming, and Sive's companions, not seeing her reaction but only his warm greeting, relaxed in the knowledge that he was no stranger after all. The green eyes took them in, crinkling in amusement. "I'm very sorry, ladies, to have taken you by surprise. I did not mean to alarm you."

Courtesies completed, he spoke now only to Sive.

"I've just been to speak to your father."

Sive knew with dreadful certainty why he was there. Yet she heard herself say stupidly, as though compelled to act out the charade, "What about?"

He offered a fond, slightly reproachful smile. "Why, about you, my dear. I have asked him for your hand."

So it had come. Fear roiled in Sive's stomach and poured into her legs, turning them weak and watery. She barely understood his next words.

"Your father received me graciously and acknowledges that my offer for a bride price is very generous. But he says he must discuss it with you first. So I will give you a few days to consider."

This was Far Doirche's way, Sive was learning. He painted a picture of gentle courtesy, but behind it lay the threat, hard and inescapable.

Far's smile took in the other women now, enlisting their support. Then the green eyes fell on Sive, drilling into her.

"I hope very much that you will favor my suit, and that I will return to good news."

With a quick nod of farewell, he strode down the road behind them.

Sive's friends burst into excited chatter.

"He's so handsome!"

"Where did you meet him?"

"Will you say yes?"

Sive did not reply. Mechanically, she bent down and began to gather up her fallen bouquet. When she finished, she risked a glance back at the Dark Man.

The laneway was empty.

YOUR FATHER RECEIVED ME GRACIOUSLY. Was the response genuine, or had her father been stalling for time? One look at Derg's worried face in the doorway told her that he did, indeed, know what Far Doirche was.

"Thanks be you are back," he said. "You are in danger, daughter."

"I know," she replied. "I met him on the road."

"Did he touch you?" Derg's voice was sharp with anxiety.

"No." Sive was confused at his long exhalation of relief. What did that matter? Derg took her arm and pulled her into the house.

"Come and sit with me. We are backed into a foxhole, with little time to find our way out."

She had barely made contact with the cushions when he began.

"How do you know this man?"

"I don't know him," she protested. "I have hardly exchanged two words with him. But he noticed my singing."

"At Bodb Dearg's?"

Sive nodded, her throat going tight with the memory. "He warned Elatha away from me."

Her father sighed again. "So that was it. Sive, do you know what he is?"

"Elatha calls him the Dark Man and says he is a sorcerer. He said Far Doirche must want to use my voice for his own ends."

Her father was grim now, his pleasing voice gone harsh. "That must never happen. You must never be in his thrall."

The word alarmed her. "Why do you say that—in his *thrall*?"

"Sive, you would not be his wife. You would be his slave, your own will overpowered by his dark arts. You have seen his hazel staff?"

Sive thought back to their encounter on the road. Yes, he had carried a staff.

"With a touch of that rod, Far Doirche can bend a person to his will," Derg continued. "Only the oldest and mightiest among us have the power to resist. He is required to leave the staff outside when he attends gatherings like Bodb Dearg's or enters a dwelling place, and so far he has complied. Otherwise it would not be long until the people simply scattered at his approach or met it with a host of spears. He wears a pleasant, ordinary face and so there are still many who do not know his true nature."

"The way he asked you so properly for me."

Derg nodded, his lean face tight and angry. "As if he would hesitate to take what is not given."

He leaned forward, underlining the import of his next words.

"You must understand this. With you, he could subdue his victims by the dozens—perhaps hundreds. His reach would become as long as the distance your voice carries. He could approach a gathering of chieftains and send you singing before him."

Sive saw it now, pictured the horror of it. She would sing for her master, whether she wished it or not, and powerful men would fall down in sweet sleep. The Dark Man would be free to wander among them with his hazel rod, turning them into an army of unwilling slaves. How many men would he harvest, traveling from one corner of Tir na nOg to the other, before word began to arrive ahead of them and some defense devised?

Tears stung her eyes, and she pressed them back, along with the despairing inner voice that whispered, *There is no escape. This will destroy you.* There was no time for weeping or despair, not now. Not yet.

"Will our own king not protect me?" Sive asked, though she knew if her salvation were that simple her father would long since have suggested it. Instead, he shook his head sadly.

"If I were blood kin to the king, one of his *sept*, then he would be obliged to come to your defence at my request. But he would not prevail. There are none in this sidhe with the power to resist Far Doirche's enchantments and disguises."

Sive wanted to hide her face in her mother's skirts, as she had when she was a tiny child frightened by a wasp or a clap of thunder. But Grian was far away, visiting her sister

Niamh at their father Manannan's Underwave palace, and Sive was far beyond the little girl whose greatest worry was an insect sting.

"How did you get on with Bodb?"

Sive forced herself to come back to the moment and her father's voice.

"He welcomed me graciously enough, but we didn't really speak after that." Not the answer Derg had been hoping for, she saw.

"And Far associates you with that place. He may expect you to seek protection there." Derg straightened up. "Well then, I think your course is clear. You must go to your grandfather. Manannan has many enchantments and protections against unwanted guests. He holds me in poor esteem and has been cold to your mother since she left Bodb, but he does not bar her from his house, and I am sure he will not turn his back on her blameless child. You will be safe in Underwave.

"But you must leave now. When Far comes, I will tell him you are walking the woods and delay him as long as I can. But the time may come, if I cannot escape his rod, that I am forced to tell the truth. By then you must be long gone."

Sive Remembers

I never made it to my grandfather's hidden island, nor even to the strand where the entrance to his undersea realm can be found. I had hardly traveled for half a day and was only beginning to emerge from the fog of confusion and fear, the hasty preparations and instructions, the tearful goodbye. Would I ever see my father again, or would we be forever divided by my grandfather's enmity on the one side and Far Doirche's lust on the other?

I never dreamed that he would find me so fast. We were a little way into a series of deeply wooded hills, cutting across the northern edge of the mountains that lie between my home and the coast. The track was loamy and soft, and we had slowed our horses so they could pick their way down a steep slope.

The thunder of the hoofbeats pounding up behind us was paralyzing. Like a scream in the black of night, it was a sound of pure terror. Laisren and Ciaran—the two men who escorted me, trusted friends of my father—did not expect pursuit. They believed, as I did, that we had at least a couple of days before Far Doirche returned, that we would easily reach Baile's Strand well ahead of him. They pulled up their horses in cautious curiosity and waited to see who rode in such haste.

But I knew, knew as surely as if his rod loomed over my head.

I kicked my horse hard, making him leap to the bottom of the gully and take the next slope at a laboring run. But where was I running to? Not far ahead, I knew, the land opened up, returning to gently rolling plains and light woods all the way to the hill of Tara. It would not be long until I was overtaken.

At the top of the slope, I reined in, pulled my horse a little off the track and risked a look back.

Far Doirche, astride a huge war horse in full trappings, was leaning over the saddle to wrench his spear from Ciaran's chest.

Laisren was on foot, in combat with Far's companion—a mighty man in full war harness. I was heartsick, but there was no time for tears, for even as I watched, Far seated his spear and looked up the track to where I lingered. A triumphant smile creased his face and his eyes sought mine, but this time I looked away before he could trap me. I slid from my saddle.

"Remember," my father had told me, "your voice is not your only power. He cannot command the wild beasts."

I was afraid I would have trouble turning, but once a thing is learned well, it is never forgotten. In a heartbeat the world turned amber and brown, and the acrid smell of blood filled my nostrils. I had no need for track nor horse. My own legs were long and strong and could penetrate the deepest forest. I turned south and east, into the mountains, and ran until my legs trembled and the breath rasped in my lungs, until it was too dark for even a deer to see.

SEVEN

For four days Sive wandered the mountains. Avoiding the bare summits that would allow a keen eye to spot the movement of a young doe picking her way through the heather, she kept instead to the heavily wooded slopes and ravines where sunlight hardly penetrated. At night she sheltered inside the skirts of sprawling junipers or behind deadfalls, ears flared, starting at every sound. She had never spent a night alone. Now she knew the uneasy sleep of a creature who is hunted day and night, for she heard the wolves singing to the moon and realized there was more than Far Doirche to be wary of.

Hunger finally drove her from the silent dark pine forest where she felt safest, to more open ground. It had become a constant, gnawing pain, as if her body was trying to eat itself from the inside. Food had always been an entertainment and a pleasure for Sive; now she was horrified to find herself light-headed and weak, to realize that her very survival hinged on clumps of grass and fallen hazelnuts.

She followed the flank of the mountain to its lower slopes, where the pines gave way to oak, birch and hazel trees. The woodland grew busy with wildlife: red squirrels stuffed their cheeks with nuts and seeds, robins gorged on hawthorn berries, hare crouched trembling under the ferns. Sive found a trail punctuated with delicate hoofprints and deer scat and followed it cautiously. She cropped tall autumn grass at the edge of a clearing, not noticing how odd it was to find such sweet relief in a patch of weeds, thinking only of filling her stomach.

In the late afternoon the land opened up to reveal a lake nestled between the mountains. In its waters the pale blue of the sky became a deep, brilliant indigo, startling in Sive's vision after the tans and ochers of the woods. So peaceful and lovely it was that Sive could not resist its pull. She yearned to wade and drink in those blue waters, with the perfect reflection of the mountain peaks wavering about her legs, as though the hardships she had suffered could be washed away with the dried mud crusting her hooves.

She was halfway to the water when she smelled smoke, and no brushfire either. It was the tang of peat she smelled, and that meant a hearth. Heart tripping with mingled excitement and fear, Sive scanned the shore of the lake.

A thin plume of smoke rose into the sky, just a little way around the shore. Sive raised her muzzle and flared her nostrils, searching for the scent of the person who had made it. There—the faintest whiff, but a person, clearly. Just one, it seemed, not a settlement. Far Doirche. Sive almost leapt away at the mere thought, but something made her wait. Yet it must be him. Why else would a person be in such a lonely spot? Him, or a hunter. In either case she should be far, far away.

She jumped at a sudden bang, the skin over her shoulders rippling in alarm. A door? Was there a dwelling hidden behind the lakeside trees? Now the scent came clearly to her as the person—the *woman!*—was caught in the breeze. Sive watched, intent and curious, fear forgotten, and was rewarded with the sight of a small figure approaching the water's edge. A woman, definitely, with a bucket in one hand which she filled at the shore. She was bent, though, and walked slowly. Sive wondered if she favored some injury.

Moments later the woman had disappeared from view, and the peat smoke grew rich with the scent of frying onions. Sive's mouth filled with saliva even as the deer part of her urged her away.

Four days, and there had been no sign of pursuit. She must be far away from the Dark Man by now. Surely she would be safe here, at least for a time.

Even as she made the decision, her body was dissolving, streaming into the upright, slim shape of a woman. Green leapt into her sight, the lakeside foliage glowing in the slanting sunlight, and Sive straightened herself luxuriously. Such a pleasure, it was, just to take on her own true form and walk once again on two legs. Nervously, she patted her hands over her head and smoothed her gown. All seemed to be as it was before she changed, unaffected by her days in the wild.

With a deep breath, Sive began the walk around the shoreline.

"I HAVE HER!"

Far Doirche clutched the amber pendant hanging on his chest and closed his eyes, head cocked as though listening to a faraway whisper. "You've traveled far, little deer," he murmured.

Then the green eyes snapped open, and their fierce will bored into Oran.

"She has turned, but she is deep in the mountains."

"Shall I saddle your horse, master?" Oran's heart had been stirred by Sive's unexpected escape, and he was filled now with pity. His master had plucked a long auburn hair from Sive's shoulder at their roadside meeting. That hair, preserved in resin and held against Far Doirche's skin, would lead the sorcerer to the poor girl whenever she took her own shape.

Oran had long ago learned to keep his expression neutral and submissive. He did not show his dismay when his master waved away his suggestion with contempt.

"Horse is too slow. There is barely a footpath to Glendalough. I will require *other* means."

Far Doirche's features burned with predatory anticipation.

"Lay the fire and then bring me one of the captive crows. I will travel on the ashes of its wings."

THE HOUSE WAS SMALL and poor, a squat round building with white walls and a tall thatched roof. Sive paused before the entrance, taking in the lack of windows and crude workmanship. Why would anyone choose to live like this?

Still, the memory of frying onions lingered in Sive's nostrils. She glanced up at the smoke rising from the thatch, unaware of how she flared her nostrils, questing after an aroma that was too far for her human senses to capture.

She was saved from knocking or calling when the door abruptly opened, releasing a cloud of cooking odor, the onions joined now by meat and herbs. Sive stared at the woman standing on the sill.

She was as small and hunched as her house, her face wrinkled like a dried-out apple. Her hair was coarse and gray, a color Sive had never seen on any person. She had heard that a decay like this plagued the children of the Gael as they grew old, and wondered if this woman could be a visitor from the mortal lands. The woman laughed at Sive's expression, the sound musical and merry.

"You wonder at my appearance. I must say I wonder at yours as well. It is not every day a woman wanders out of the wilds for a neighborly visit!"

She studied Sive up and down, her gaze sharp within the deep folds of skin. "It is a rough walk here from anywhere, yet you look as fresh as a spring bluebell. Though your eyes tell a different tale. Come in, so." Sive's strange host stood back to make room, and Sive ducked into the dim house. "We'll share a meal, and then perhaps we'll share our mysteries."

HER NAME WAS MURIGEN, and she saved Sive the trouble of finding a polite way of asking why she lived in such a place.

"A hag in a run-down hut," she said as she eased herself onto a wooden bench. "I don't suppose you've ever seen the like."

"I haven't," Sive admitted, pulling herself briefly away from her wooden bowl. Food had never tasted this good, she was certain of it.

"I have a fine enough form, and no lack of lodgings. But there are times when I grow weary of the din of the world, and of the attentions of men. Then I come here, to these waters that are my charge."

Murigen flashed an amused smile, gesturing down her body. "I learned this from the mortal lands. When the women grow gray and wrinkled, the men leave them alone."

Not me, thought Sive. Unless she could rip her voice from her very throat, one man would never leave her alone.

Murigen's eyes fastened on Sive, alert as a bird's. "Ah, now. There is a bleak look. What is it that haunts those pretty eyes and sends you to roam the mountains?"

There was a power pulsing through this woman. Sive had sensed it from the moment she entered the little house. A thin bright thread of hope unfurled in her breast. Perhaps there was true shelter here.

"There is a man," she began. "A sorcerer."

A wrinkled finger, thrust in the air, stopped her words. Murigen tipped her head to one side, her features attentive, as though she listened—but not to Sive.

"Someone is here."

"Someone—where?" Sive was on her feet, looking wildly around the dim cabin, but Murigen flapped her hand toward the bench and Sive perched, reluctantly, at its edge. He couldn't be here, so quickly. He couldn't.

Murigen turned to Sive. She did not look pleased. "I have protections on this place. I know when its borders are passed. And this is the second time today that a person has appeared on my land well past the place where I should have sensed it!"

"Who—?" There was no interrupting her. She was intent, in charge.

"This sorcerer," demanded Murigen. "Does he hunt you?"

Sive nodded. There was no need for more.

"Then it is him. You must flee now, for he is not far off." She was walking as she spoke, pulling Sive to her feet and out the door, bent no longer but brisk and strong. The bright eyes fixed on Sive again.

"I assume you have better clothing for the wilderness than that silk dress."

Again Sive nodded.

"Then change into it, and fly!" Her brisk manner softened, and the gnarled fingers rested on Sive's shoulder. "My good wishes go with you, child."

Sive's shoulders crawled with the need to change, but she held off.

"Murigen, be careful. He has a staff—"

A bark of laughter cut her off.

"He cannot harm me with his little stick. I am far too old for such nonsense."

Sive's heart, already beating too fast, tripped into a canter, the hope unfurling into a bright ribbon.

"Then can you—could I not—?" Her words were halting and incoherent, unable somehow to ask now the possibility loomed. But Murigen understood, was already shaking her head.

"I am sorry, child, truly. I cannot protect you. Your man has no power over the likes of me, but neither can I stop him. My business is with the lakes and rivers, not with people. If he were foolish enough to swim in these waters, then yes. He would have some trouble, I think, were I to call forth the ancient creature who lurks in their secret depths..."

She became brisk again. "But he won't. And you must be off. I'll see you leave no prints to guide him."

The panic of the hunt surged in Sive's chest, and with it came the deer. The air rippled as her form streamed into hooves and legs and thrusting muzzle. The pale green silk was gone, replaced with a sleek auburn coat still daubed with the last remnants of a fawn's white spots.

The deer sprang up the mountainside, pale rump flashing. Murigen stayed until the noise in the underbrush was almost too faint to hear; then she stumped into her house to tidy up. The sorcerer would be in sight at any moment. Just as well he find her at home—with the remains of *one* bowl of stew.

EIGHT

S ive jolted awake, her body trembling with alarm before her mind understood the reason. Then the sound that had threaded through her dreams came clear: hounds. Their music was faint in the still air, floating up the mountainside from far away. But it was Sive they sang for, of that she had no doubt. The Dark Man was on the hunt.

Day after day the hounds quested for her. The mountains were vast, and at first it was not hard to stay clear of them. But each day more packs added their clamor to the air, and no matter how many false trails they followed after other deer, Far Doirche always set them back to their true quarry. It seemed to Sive the baying voices rang out from all directions now and she began to feel the net Far had cast about her feet slowly drawing tighter. She would have to go down and break past the dogs while there were still gaps between the packs.

Yet something else sought her on the lower slopes. It was the time of the rut, and not even the onslaught of hunters could stop the stags from gathering their harems. Their bellowing cries added a deep bass counterpoint to the yelping hounds. They guarded their does jealously, herding them to what seemed the safest spots, challenging any stag that dared approach. The first time Sive attempted to slip past the dog packs and escape into the long, tractless stretch of the mountains, she all but ran into a group of does huddled nervously together. They stamped and twitched their ears at the sound of the hunt but stayed in their group. Then Sive saw the stag. On a high outcrop of rock, a powerful form topped with a mighty rack of antlers, he was a magnificent sight. And his entire attention was fixed on her, as predatory as a wolf. The thick shoulders and great shaggy throat ruff seemed to swell as he took her in.

Sive fled back up the mountain, not resting until the dark pines swallowed her.

THE MAGPIE'S WINGS flashed with startling white patches as it swooped through the gloom. Woodtits, treecreepers, squirrels—there were many in the pines, busily digging insects from under the bark or prying seeds from the cones. Magpies, though, favored the richer offerings of mixed woods and open hills.

Even through a deer's eyes it was a handsome bird, and Sive paused in her miserable attempt to browse on the fungus growing from a fallen log to follow its flight. But the bird checked sharply and dipped down to perch on a dead branch thrust from the log. It cocked its head and stared at her with one shiny black eye.

Nosy thing, thought Sive. Find your own feast. But then she thought twice and stepped back. Lacking both a deer's instinct and a mother's training, she did not know enough about what was edible. If the magpie sampled her fungus, that would be one thing she could eat without fear of poisoning.

But the magpie did not move. It simply stared at her, first from one side and then the other, and suddenly Sive's heart was pounding, not daring to believe yet somehow certain all the same. And sure enough the space where the magpie had been was rippling and blurring with color. In an instant, her father stood before her, the smell of him so familiar though a hundred times stronger to her animal senses, his shape and stance so well-remembered though his features were strangely blurred in her eyes.

And she was streaming into her own shape without even willing it, thinking only of rushing into his arms. But his urgent shout rang on the air.

"Sive, NO! He will be upon us if you change! You must stay as you are!"

"I can't!" She was sobbing, caught in the stream of shifting energies, so full of need.

"Only for a moment, Sive, I promise you. You must not change here."

Everything within her was rushing toward him, but she trusted his word. She closed her eyes and forced herself back to animal form. The pain of it was shocking—not a liquid flowing transformation, but flesh and bone ripped and shoved into place. She gritted the jaws that had already lengthened away from the hinge of the joint, caught between mouth and muzzle, and willed herself to endure it.

"Brave girl." Derg spoke softly, not wanting to excite a new flare of emotion that might betray her. She trembled and panted already from the effort of the change.

"Come with me, dear one. There is a stream not far from here. Far Doirche is not all-powerful after all. Not yet."

FAR DOIRCHE HAD been patient and pleasant for days, but now he rounded on the man who brought him the latest downed deer, mangled but alive.

"Am I paying you to feed all of Tir na nOg? Can you not tell the difference between a buck and a doe, at least?" He kicked at the offending beast, who struggled where it lay but was too badly wounded to rise.

The hunter blanched and took a hasty step back from the angry druid. "Of course, Far Doirche, but the hounds don't distinguish. You asked to see all our catch, but I can instruct them to weed out the…" The man's voice trailed off as he risked at glance at his employer.

Far clutched at the pendant at his neck, his eyes vague and faraway, the buck forgotten. "Here she comes at last," he murmured. But his knowing smile faded away. His brows knotted; his knuckles whitened from the pressure of his grip. With something very like a snarl he released the amber talisman.

"Our vixen is a tease," he said. Already composed, his voice smooth as tallow, he gave the hunter an easy smile that caused the man to take another cautious step backward. "Luckily there is no end to men who enjoy hunting, especially for a price. One way or another, I will have her."

THEY WADED INTO the deepest water they could find, and then at Derg's urging Sive sank down onto her haunches.

"This will buy us a little time," he said. "Less of you to track. Let me see you now, daughter, but take care to stay covered."

In a heartbeat she was with him. She gasped as the icy water pierced her thin skin, and then as her father's face came clear and he waded forward to embrace her, she was weeping, sobbing into his chest like a little girl waking from a bad dream.

But already he was talking, his voice low and urgent.

"We must be quick. Even now he will know you have taken your right form again."

"How can he?" Twice now Far Doirche had seemed to know exactly where she was.

"He has something of yours." Sive shook her head against him, but Derg insisted. "He must have. It could be something you are unaware of, as small as a hair. But it draws him like a beacon."

Derg released her and stepped back, so they could see each other's faces. "Manannan taught me this trick. The formlessness of the water will confuse Far Doirche and slow him down."

Derg nodded at her unspoken question, but his mouth drew into an angry line. "Manannan saw me, for your sake, and for your mother's. But he will not set himself against the Dark Man, not until he is directly threatened."

Sive shook her head in baffled frustration. "But isn't that just what will happen?"

"It is, and by then the battle will be that much more perilous. But Far has put it about that it is I who have cursed you with the deer's form, to punish you for defying me. He says I set myself against a love-match between you and him." He acknowledged Sive's indignant cry with a bitter smile. "Aye, a ridiculous pretense, as Manannan knows well. But until there is proof he will not challenge it. The old ones do not concern themselves with the love-knots of girls. That is a father's duty, or a husband's."

Her father's features twisted. "You'd be better off if you were Bodb Dearg's daughter, and that's the hard truth of it."

Before Sive could say anything—and her mind was in such a turmoil that she did not know what words she would find—her father hurried on.

"There is not much time. The Dark Man will not be delayed very long by this ruse. Sive, there is one thing that may be of help to you. You know when Manannan drew the veil between Tir na nOg and the mortal world, he left doorways where those of us who wish to travel in our old lands may pass through."

Sive nodded. She had never thought much about it, but she knew there were ways to get there.

"There are other openings between our worlds, many of them. Cracks and holes and burrows and streams traveled these many centuries by the wild creatures. They do not distinguish between worlds, and so they pass freely between them."

He leaned forward, intent now. "Sive, when we are changed we can pass through as well. I have done it. If you have need, you can enter the mortal world and Far will not be able to follow you—not through the same portal. He must use the doorways Manannan created. I do not know if he will be able to track you in the mortal lands as he does here, but he will certainly be delayed in his pursuit.

"Wherever you flee, you must seek out these places. They may save you when nothing else can."

"But—" Sive was overwhelmed. Time hurried on like the stream through her fingers, and Far Doirche's shadow loomed. Her mind was a jumble of frantic questions. She grabbed at the most insistent.

"How will I find them? I don't know what to look for."

"Once you find the first few, you will learn to sense them," her father assured her. "They will begin to draw you as you pass by.

"There are many in these mountains," he added. "I will lead you to the one I have found. But we must not linger here, daughter. Become a deer, now, before the Dark Man is upon us."

Sive Remembers

It was the last thing my father told me that put me into despair. I had changed by then, and could not speak, and so perhaps he did not know the hopelessness that came over me with this last, cruel fact.

"Be wary, daughter," he urged gravely. "Do not think your red coat makes you invisible."

Why not? I wondered, but could not say. But he answered all the same.

"I did you no favor, it seems, leading you toward your change so young, and for that I am sorry. For you have kept the form you first took—a nearly grown doe still carrying the last spots of the fawn."

I remember craning my head around, trying to get a look at my own flank. I might just as well be marked with woad. Even the late fawns had taken on an adult coat by now. If every deer in these mountains were gathered together, and I in the midst of them, Far Doirche would know me. Woman or deer, he would track me down.

The cave Derg had shown me was a long, winding crevice into the rocky heart of the mountain. I imagined I could feel something as we neared the end—the way you can sense the coming dawn, though the world is dark as deepest night, or the way you know, even with your eyes shut, if you are deep under the water or near the surface. This was like being near the surface, a sense of being about to break through into air and light despite the close, dark confines of the cave. Or perhaps I did imagine it.

In any case, once my father led me back to the cave's mouth and flew off through the dappled woods, despair took hold and with it a wild need to bolt. That was the deer driving me. When there is nothing left, you simply run.

But there was no place in my homeland where I could hide. No disguise that would hold, no sanctuary I could reach ahead of the Dark Man.

One great bound took me back inside the cave's granite walls. Quickly, without thought or plan, I retraced the steep narrow path to its end. I hesitated, but only for a heartbeat, before the black pool that lay silent before me. I could smell the water better than I could see it. It seemed a certain death, but my father had said that water led to the mortal lands, and yes, I could feel it beyond the depths. It called to me, for was Eire not our old homeland as well?

If I died, it would not be the worst thing that could happen. With a scrape and clatter of hooves on wet rock, I threw myself in.

THE BLACK WATER SUCKED her down, the undertow strong as the ocean's pull despite the stillness of the pool's surface.

Sive's limbs thrashed instinctively against it, but she could make no headway. Her fate was with the water now—to drown or to be somehow delivered to a new land.

Her lungs burned; her ears pounded. The need for air grew beyond refusing, and she was on the very brink of the great gasping breath that would bring water rushing into her lungs and death on its heels.

And then the pool released her, shooting her up to the surface, and it was life that flooded into her after all. With the last of her strength, she hauled herself over the slippery ledge and lay, flanks heaving, on the cold rock.

It hadn't worked. There was magic in that pool—Derg had been right about that. But it had spit her back to the same dank, tight cave, to the very ledge she had jumped from, as if it knew she was an imposter. She could not pass through.

Sive lay a long time in the dark. Doing nothing, thinking nothing—it was a relief. She could give up, hide in here till she starved. Or go back to the dark pool and this time let it take her.

And yet...she had fought to live, in that water. Gasped in the sweet air like a newborn baby when it was returned to her. She was not ready to die. Gingerly, her mind began to stir. It began to search, once again, for a way out. She would have to try again to break through the ring of hunters before it drew any tighter. She would roam the mountains, always on the move, or work her way northeast and try once more to reach Manannan's stronghold. Surely he would not refuse her face to face? She shook her head. Far Doirche would expect that, would be waiting to corner her on the strand. Bodb. She would cross the country, ask Daireann to intercede for her.

Such faint hopes. She did not believe any of them could succeed. But she could not—yet—lie down and die, and so she gathered herself up and picked her way through the narrow passage back to the open air.

She heard the rain before she saw it: drumming rain and lashing wind that made the trees groan and snap. At the mouth of the crevice she stared, astonished, at the fury that raged over the mountains.

Sive thought she knew rain. It showered down often, watering the crops and keeping the land green and fresh. She knew wind, as well, from the gentle summer breeze that dried the sweat on her brow and freshened her chamber to the crisp, stiff wind that blew the leaves from the trees in autumn. But this!

This rain lashed down so hard she could hardly see through it, flung from thick gray cloud that smothered the earth. It drove into the cave where she sheltered, blown almost sideways by a wind that roared through the mountains like a mad beast.

And freezing. Even in her stiff fur hide, she felt the bite of that wind, the rain like ice needles in her face.

The crack and the flash came almost together, lightning forking through the gloom only a short way down the slope.

Sive jumped at the noise, her nose wrinkling at the bitter, burnt smell.

Coat shivering and rippling with alarm, she retreated back into the passage and huddled in a dry spot. It would not be dry for long, not with the amount of water already flowing down the sloping passage.

Sive had never known a storm like this. Weather that could kill a person, violent as a battlefield—it was not part of her world.

Wherever she was, it was not Tir na nOg.

NINE

Winter came to the mortal lands, and Sive still wandered, afraid to leave her animal form lest she alert Far Doirche. The full moon lit the earth as before, but it was not the gentle wash of light Sive remembered. This moon had a fierce white face, so cold and distant its only intent might be to make a young woman trapped in a deer's flesh feel smaller and more alone than she had ever imagined possible. Gazing at it summoned a tearless mute grief that verged on despair. Sive learned to keep her eyes down on clear nights.

Through that first hard winter, Sive thought only of returning home. Her plan, such as it was, was to travel far away from anywhere Far Doirche might be seeking her, taking enough time in the journey that he might even give up his fruitless quest. Then she would find a doorway to Tir na nOg and slip back in.

What would happen next—how she would regain her own form without summoning the Dark Man's attention—she could not say.

Coming out of the mountains through a gap that led her northwest between wind-scoured slopes carpeted in tough brown heather, Sive came to a river valley dotted with farms and small round houses. She was spotted and hunted once as she skirted its edge, searching for a place to cross. But her speed was too great for men on foot and their few hounds, and she soon left them behind. It was not being eaten that worried her so much as the fear that news would spread of the strange doe who kept her spots in winter. For there were many among her people who walked in the mortal lands from time to time and who might carry such a rumor back with them to Far's ear.

It was a dark, wet, cold country. As far as Sive was concerned, the sons of the Gael were welcome to it. She saw them sometimes, wrapped in cloaks and blankets, bent into the wind or hunched under the rain. The winter she knew—brisk and fresh, with a dusting of snow to sparkle in the sun and dress the world in a clean white beauty—was a thing glimpsed only on rare days.

Her goal was the northwest corner of the country, as far as possible from anyplace she had ever been in her own world. She traveled blindly, never sure of her route.

The geography of Tir na nOg and Eire might be similar, but Sive's knowledge of the land was founded on roads and settlements more than natural landmarks. She avoided human dwellings except when hunger tempted her into the orchards or fields, where she could scrape away the snow to reveal late windfalls or new winter barley, or when the only river crossing she could find was a manmade ford.

Eventually Sive came out of the forested hills and valleys into the empty flat interior where few people lived. It was a land broken up by lakes, rivers and wetlands, making any kind of straight route impossible. For many days she picked her way through treacherous bog, the ground spongy wet and laced with freezing waterways that might seem only a few inches deep and yet sink her to the hocks. There was little to eat and nowhere dry to sleep. When the ground finally rose enough to drain and become firm under her hooves, rushes and heather giving way first to shrubby brush and finally to woodland, she barely had strength left to search for shelter. The low sweeping branches of a yew tree caught her eye; she pushed into the hidden space within and slept.

The days were becoming longer, the cold not quite so chilling, when Sive came to a great lake, the far shore a ghostly shape in the morning mist. She traced it north all day and watched the water narrow into a long finger. The smell of human settlement teased at her nostrils: peat smoke, cattle and sheep manure, garbage. It grew strong as twilight fell, and soon she was skirting pastures dotted with sheep. Retreating into the woods, she waited for darkness.

When twilight had turned the world—and herself—into gray shadow, Sive sidled through hedgerows and river-bank willows until she came upon a little cluster of round thatched houses perched on the near side of the river that flowed into the lake's northern tip. At the water's edge, a pair of flimsy narrow boats was tied to a tiny wooden wharf. The settlement was silent, the people closed into their houses, doors barred against the cold.

Sive could have remained invisible and followed the river's course until she found a place to cross on her own. But she decided not to. There was something she had to try, something that might persuade her to stay in this rough land.

Quickly, before nerves and second thoughts could sap her resolve, she changed.

TO STAND ON TWO legs again! The pleasure of it, the sweet relief, nearly undid her. It was so long since she had been herself. Weepy and weak with emotion, Sive wrapped her arms around a willow trunk and pressed her face into its wet bark until her legs felt able to hold her.

The cold hit her next. Sharp and raw, it cut through her thin dress and bit deep into her skin.

If the Dark Man could track her here in Eire, how long would she have? She had no wish to be trapped in a tiny hut.

But she had to find out, and she could not stay unsheltered in the winter night, shaking like an aspen leaf.

Outside the door of the largest house—a building Sive might mistake for a storage shed in her own land—she took a deep breath. "Grant me my father's easy tongue," she prayed, and knocked firmly.

"Aye, hold on!" a deep voiced boomed from within. The door scraped open abruptly, the voice already demanding, "What is it, then?"

The words dried into astonished silence as the man regarded her. Sive's first impression was of strength— broad shoulders, broad face, thick brown hair. Yet as the man took in her delicate gown, her milky skin unlined by age or hardship, his eyes turned wary. And Sive, in turn, became frightened, realizing she knew nothing of these people. Did they even honor the laws of hospitality? Would they drive her away—or worse?

The man did neither. Instead, he turned his head toward the dark interior and bellowed, "Da! You'd best come."

There was no need to call. Peering over the wide shoulder, Sive could see a man already rising. She had a confused glimpse of others too—women, children—all silent and staring.

This was an old one, she realized. His shoulders stooped, hair grizzled and wiry and thin at the front, his face deeply etched. He looked inferior in every way to the strapping young man who had opened the door, yet it was he who would decide on her welcome.

One glance and he became brisk.

"You are half-dead with cold! Come in so, and we will speak in the warmth."

Gratefully, Sive slipped over the threshold. The young man pulled the door shut behind her.

"Mara! Your cloak for the lady!"

A girl with wide gray eyes, not yet a woman but tall, jumped up from the pot she was tending. She approached Sive with her eyes cast down, holding out the cloak by her fingertips.

Sive thanked her gravely and drew the coarse wool about her shoulders. It was threadbare and in need of cleaning, but she snuggled into it as though it were the softest down.

"Now," said the old one, reclaiming her attention. "I am Maine, and this is my son Brogan." Both gave an awkward bob of the head, as though they were not much practiced at it. "You are welcome here, and if there is anything you have need of you have only to say the word, and if it is in my power you shall have it."

Sive thought the woman at the fire—Brogan's wife, perhaps—looked distinctly alarmed at these words. But no one disputed them, and so she took courage and spoke.

"I am Sive, and I thank you for your kindness. I—" She faltered and tried again. She had already decided she could not risk telling anyone her true plight. But there was no credible way to explain herself otherwise.

"I was traveling by night and missed my path." She reached into her hair to pull out one of the gold pins that held the front pieces off her face and held it out in her palm. "I would gladly pay for food and a night's shelter with this."

She had said the wrong thing. Maine's face darkened with anger.

"We have no great riches here, but we have never yet been so poor that we would charge a stranger for shelter. Why would you expect it?"

Sive hastened to apologize. "I have traveled far and do not know your ways. I had no wish to offend."

He softened at once, and the look on him reminded Sive of her sister's maid's words: *They say mortal men can't resist our women.*

"It is too bad you did not arrive yesterday," he said as he ushered her inside. "We killed a sheep and had a great feast with all the family." The sweep of his arm made it clear the word included the other houses in the settlement. "Today we eat leftovers, but we will do our best for you."

It was an awkward meal. The people were shy with her, and no wonder. Either they guessed that Sive was a woman of the Sidhe, or they must have thought her a madwoman, traipsing through the winter wilds in a summer gown. Either way, she thought, who could blame them for being ill at ease?

Still Maine did his best, introducing her to each of his family members: his wife and youngest daughter, and his son's wife, her baby and two small boys. The women bustled off to finish preparing dinner, and some time later the family was hunched over their wooden bowls as though eating required every scrap of their attention.

It was a coarse and unappetizing dish—chunks of mutton and turnip bobbing in gluey oatmeal. The bread was fresh and hot though, and the ale surprisingly good. Sive praised both, winning a dimple of pleasure from the women.

But there was no conversation to be had, especially after Maine ventured to ask where she was going.

"You'll have been heading to our chieftain's dun, I warrant, where you can be received in proper comfort," he said. "Did you get separated from your people somehow and veer off the main road by mistake? We can walk you back and set you on the right road on the morrow."

Sive shook her head. "I am traveling alone, and—forgive me, but I cannot reveal my destination. But if you would help me across the river, I'll be very grateful."

If there had been any doubt of her strangeness before, there was none now. Even Maine was silenced.

A winter night is long, and once they had done eating and the women had cleared away the remains, the silence became oppressive. Sive was as uneasy as any of them, her nerves drawing tight as a harpstring as the Dark Man grew in her mind. Would he come? She pictured the door banging open, the black outline of his form filling the narrow space. As deer or woman, how would she get past?

It was folly to have come here, to think of passing the night in such a cage. But she had to try. If he truly could not find her in this world, then rough and raw though it was, she would learn to live here.

The baby was unsettled, her cries all the more shrill in the small house for the unnatural quiet, and Brogan pulled out a wooden flute and began to play. The melody was simple but pleasing, relaxing them all. The baby paused, distracted by the new sound, and as her mother began to sway back and forth to the tune her cries became whimpers and she let her head drop against her mam's shoulder.

Sive had the tune by the second round and began to hum along, pleased to have something to share with her hosts. The music soothed her as nothing else could have, and the Dark Man's shadow receded. If he came, he came, and she would try her best to evade him. But she would have this bit of music in the meantime.

Lost in her thoughts, she did not realize at first that the flute had stopped and only her own voice filled the dim cabin. Embarrassed at missing the ending, she looked up with a little laugh, only to find the entire family staring white-eyed, looking as though they might bolt as one from the house.

"I'm sorry." Unsure what she was apologizing for, Sive settled for a guess. "I didn't mean to intrude on your music. It's just…it's a very long time since I have heard any, and I joined in without thinking."

More silence, until at last Maine cleared his throat and waded in. "You are a woman of the Sidhe, that is plain." Sive did not deny it. "It is well known the music of the Sidhe will drive a man mad or senseless. Is it a spell you are putting over us?"

Now it was Sive's turn to be indignant. "Would I do such a thing to people who have shown me nothing but kindness? There are some few among us who have such a skill, yes, but I was not raised to repay hospitality with ill-use of any kind." The flare of anger faded, overcome by a deep, aching sorrow. The yearning for home was a hand squeezing her heart—for her lovely, sunny house with its rich colors and soft beds, for her mother's voice twined with her own, one song rising into the morning, for the careless days of her girlhood. For people who understood her.

"I just wanted to sing," she whispered.

It was the old woman, Sarai, who put things right. She rose stiffly from her stool near the fire, walked over to Sive and laid a hand on her shoulder. Sive looked up into milky blue eyes that met hers steadily.

"Your voice is the loveliest thing I have ever heard," she said. "Will you sing to us a little longer?"

TEN

The night brought a wet, thick snow that steamed into heavy fog as soon as the sun rose.

"You cannot travel on a day like this," said Sarai. "Stay another day with us and we will have a proper guest's dinner with our kinfolk."

"Stay! Stay!" The two young boys, so shy the previous night, gambolled about Sive like puppies.

She had been true to her word, had not laced her voice with the slightest enchantment. Still, music had its own magic. An evening's singing had melted away the family's edgy caution. She was welcome now from the heart, not from a host's obligation. It was hard to turn away from that. Sive pictured herself, once again a spotted deer, vanishing into the fog. It was like ceasing to exist altogether.

And there was something else holding her here. The night had been long and anxious, Sive not daring to sleep for fear of being caught unawares. But the Dark Man had not come. Now, in the morning's cheerful bustle, Sive tried to keep a stern and cautious mind. But hope grew in her like a seedling under a rock, creeping sideways unseen until it finds the place where it can leap up toward the sun. Perhaps he truly could not see her. Perhaps he was not merely delayed but actually unaware. It would take more than a day to find out.

THERE WAS NO BUILDING in the cluster of dwellings big enough to hold everyone, so Sive spent the morning following Sarai into one dark little home after another. By midday she had met the entire sprawling family, sung to two babies and a sick, bedridden grandfather, and sampled many bowls of tea and ale.

It was not clear to her where "dinner with the kinfolk" was to take place. Though the fog had lifted enough that the houses no longer looked like wavering illusions, wind and intermittent bursts of rain made it even more unpleasant outside.

Nonetheless, a pig culled from the herd soon hung spitted over a fire in the cooking shed while the women set themselves to baking and stewing. The children, gleeful at the prospect of two big dinners so close together, were put to work as well, but that did not keep them from wrestling and teasing and filling the air with their high spirits.

Sive helped where she could, hoping this extravagance—for so it evidently was—would not compromise the family's winter stores. But through it all she also kept watch. The Dark Man, if he was coming, must be near.

Sive Remembers

They hung blankets on the woven wattle walls of the cookhouse to keep out the wind, and set the food out right there. Their very best, it was, yet poor compared to what I ate every day at home. But it meant so much more, for I had seen how they toiled to provide it.

A few of the young men stayed in the cookhouse, eating by the fire, but most of us went to one house or another to find better comfort. Sarai led me to a house crowded with women, all of them gossiping and laughing and arguing. They went quiet for a bit when I entered, but it did not take them long to start up again.

I could see well enough that there were jealousies and resentments among them. But I saw too the strength of the bonds they shared—it shimmered among them like an invisible rope, twining one to another. They knew each other's troubles and joys, shared jokes and stories reaching back to their childhood. In that warm, noisy gabble of women, my own solitude seemed unbearable.

BROGAN PADDLED STEADILY, drawing the tippy coracle ever closer to the far bank. The strange woman of the Sidhe was leaving them, and an uncomfortable mix of relief, regret and worry—for how could anyone, from any land, travel through winter slush and mud with nothing but those dainty scraps of cloth on their feet?—warred within him. Still he kept his mind to his task, for the Shannon had strong currents beneath its smooth surface and a dunking mid-river could be the death of them both.

Sive huddled in the front facing Brogan, wrapped in the old blanket Maine had pressed on her.

"Almost there, m'lady." He gestured with his chin to the little strand where the coracles could be pulled right up on shore. A jetty had never seemed necessary, not with that shelf of gravelly sand, but Brogan wished for one now. He did not, as a rule, cross the river in winter, so he had never minded wading through a few inches of water to haul up the boat. Today it would be an icy soaking.

Sive twisted around in her seat to see for herself. She scanned the shore and then leapt to her feet with a cry. The coracle rocked wildly, but Brogan's sharp instructions died in his throat when he saw her face. The color blanched from her cheeks, eyes wild. Her mouth worked, but no words escaped.

Brogan checked the shore himself in alarm. A single figure came into view, walking along the track that led from the strand to the Western Road. He raised a hand casually, it seemed in greeting.

Brogan's eyesight blurred, fragmenting the woman before him into a jumble of fleeting images. He squinted but could not bring her into focus. Then a violent heave threw the coracle out of control. Brogan flung himself low across the gunnels as the little boat spun and bucked, on the very brink of capsize.

It took only moments for the danger to pass, but when Brogan looked up the woman was gone. Fallen in! Frantic, he searched the surface of the water for her.

A deer swam strongly north against the current, already too far to catch up. Brogan gaped, his body slack with shock, unable to accept what his eyes told him.

An angry shout brought him out of his daze. The fellow on the far shore had reached the riverbank now, was in fact running north along the strand, shaking his walking staff and yelling at the deer.

"Swim fast, Sive," Brogan whispered. Somehow the stranger's threats made the words believable. Whoever that man was, he would be hard-pressed to follow her, for where the little strand ended, a head-high thicket of gorse grew right to the water's edge, and a little after that, where the river rounded a bend, a tumble of great rocks blocked the way.

Brogan turned the coracle around and began paddling back to his jetty. He did not intend to give the stranger any chance to commandeer his boat.

THE WINTER PASSED and another, and the third whispered its approach in the frosty autumn night, and still Sive wandered. She stood on the windy cliffs at the edge of the western sea, browsed the lower slopes of the wild north country mountains, slipped like mist through the orchards and pastures of great chieftains. She even watched the sun rise over a strand, which, if she had only known, could have led her to her grandfather's undersea island.

She did go back to her homeland once. She found the portal by accident: a crack gouged into the side of a great mountain that looked as though its top had been lopped off with a giant sword. A breath, a feeling, a smell? Something caught her attention as she passed by, and she remembered the same sensation from her first escape from Tir na nOg. It seemed a gift of fate, and she took it.

But it was worse, being home. Though the weather was kinder and food plentiful, the pain and loneliness were more cruel. The pull of her sidhe, and her family, were so terribly strong. Helpless to stop, she began traveling east, picturing in her mind the string of hills, the rich rolling fields at their skirts and the flat peat bog stretched out behind. If she could just have a glimpse of her house, or spot a familiar face on the road...such foolishness.

It was herself that was seen, long before she was anywhere near Sidhe Ochta Cleitigh, and it was almost a relief to have to pull her thoughts away from her homesickness and concentrate on eluding the hunters. When the small hunting parties swelled suddenly to swarms of men and dogs, she knew the Dark Man had received word of the spotted deer he sought. She barely reached the portal in time.

She stayed in Eire after that. At least if she fell to the hunt, it would be to feed a family's hunger, not a sorcerer's ambition.

She never again risked staying in a dwelling overnight, but she did, a few times a year, allow herself a brief time in human form. To share the company of another person, a bowl of ale or the comfort of a fire—these were sharp, bittersweet pleasures.

Yet it was not loneliness but fear that made her risk attracting the Dark Man's notice and take her own form, for each day spent as a deer took her further from herself. It became difficult to remember her life as a woman. How could she picture her mother's face, when her deer eyes distinguished faces so poorly? Or recall the intricate stitches her clever fingers had embroidered, when she had no hands? She was afraid she would forget how to sing, how to speak. How to change.

ELEVEN

Daireann preened and fluttered as she waited for Far at their rendezvous. She could still hardly believe her luck, that the tall druid had turned his flattering attentions to her. He was so handsome, so courtly. The power that lay behind his gentle manners was heady and exciting, like a smooth, sweet mead that went straight to your head.

She hoped she didn't smell of horse. Far said some might find their courtship unseemly, with Sive still lost in the mortal lands, so they met at some distance from her sidhe. Daireann was happy to stay out of her father's eye for now. Still the horseback ride made it difficult to present herself at her best.

He didn't seem to notice, hurrying to help her from the horse with a murmured apology for the wait she had endured, bending low over her hand and then drinking her in with his emerald eyes before drawing her close. The little gazebo he led her to was hung with silks, lined with cushions and provisioned with an enticing array of refreshments. A brazier chased away any chill breezes that might find their way inside.

"I wish I had met you first," he said as they lay twined together in the soft nest of pillows. "I would not have wasted these past years running after the lesser beauty."

Daireann nodded archly. "I confess I never understood what you saw in her. She's a timid thing, I would think ill-suited to a great man like you."

"I know it." His grin was ruefully self-mocking. "I think she must have enchanted me." The green eyes glinted at her, glowing with intensity. "And now you have done the same."

They didn't speak of Sive again, not until more sweet encounters had been stolen and Far Doirche had delighted Daireann by begging her to become his wife.

"I hope her father will release the poor thing, once our marriage is announced," he said. "You know him—do you think he will?"

Daireann considered her reply carefully. Powerful men do not like to be crossed or gainsaid. This she had learned. But Far would not want a fool for a wife either. It was a gamble, either way.

"I doubt very much that Derg cursed her at all," she said bluntly. "He hasn't the skill. Sive, on the other hand, babbled incessantly as a child about wanting to shapeshift. Don't ask me why."

She met the green eyes head-on, allowing a spark of malicious humor into her own. "It's my belief the little fool refused you, and when you pressed your suit, turned herself into a deer to escape you. And it's no blame to you if you were angered at the slight—as if she would ever get a better offer!"

The little salute of admiration Far gave her made Daireann flush with pleasure. They would be a mighty couple.

"So," he pressed, "I still feel badly that she has endured such hardship. Do you hear from her at all? If there were some way to get the news to her, she would be free to come home."

"YES, ORAN, I MEAN you to spy on her! How clear do I have to be? Lurk by her chamber door, follow after her serving women, find some task to do where she's dining. Listen without getting caught." Far aimed a cuff at the boy's head to reinforce his words. "Now do you understand?"

Oran tried to put space between himself and the sorcerer without visibly moving his body. He failed, and the blow landed squarely on his temple. "Yes, master. I understand."

Far smiled warmly. "Good. You hear any news of Sive's whereabouts, you bring it to me."

"I will, master." Oran bowed deeply and rushed from the room.

Oran Remembers

If Daireann had revealed where Sive was, I would have told the Dark Man. I would have hated myself for it, but I could not have helped myself. I am bound to follow his commands.

But she did not. Instead she said the strangest thing to her woman.

"Imagine Sive, trotting around the mortal lands all this time. The weather there is dreadful, you know. And what could she be eating? Surely not acorns and shrubbery!"

She laughed then, tinkly and careless. "If she only knew, she has only to hop over to Finn mac Cumhail's dun. Not even Far could touch her there. I learned that from Finn himself, the day I cursed him. He said that his uncle Lugh had stretched his bright hand in protection over his dun, and no dark magic could penetrate there. He said once he made it back home, my curse would break."

She laughed again, the sound venomous this time. "Much good it did him, and he on the other side of Eire! And, now that I think of it, much good would it do Sive. I almost forgot—the great Finn mac Cumhail holds no truck with women of the Sidhe. He would not open his door to her."

I was not compelled to tell my master what I had learned, and I did not. I buried Daireann's words deep within myself, where I hoped he would not find them. And I waited for a chance to use them.

THE HOUSE SEEMED empty without the women. Derg wondered if he should close it up and take a chamber in the king's palace. He could not foresee how it would ever be safe for either of them to return, though he feared Grian might decide otherwise. She grew steadily more restive on her father's secluded island. He visited as often as he could, but even if Manannan allowed him to move in, he doubted she would be content there.

Would the Dark Man really take Grian, if he could not have Sive? Perhaps the risk was too great, even for him. Surely Manannan would stand against him, if it were his own daughter under threat.

Derg's brain would run in these circles all day if he allowed it. He was grateful for the busy day that awaited, a thousand details to arrange for the Winter Solstice games that began on the morrow.

His man poked his head into the sunroom.

"Pardon the interruption. Far Doirche asks to see you."

Derg grimaced. "Again? He has become quite the familiar face, hasn't he?"

"Indeed, sir."

Far Doirche's periodic visits no longer made Derg's heart pound in alarm. Several times a year, presumably when his travels brought him near, he stopped by to assure himself that Sive remained hidden to Derg as well as to the world.

"His hazel rod?"

"Checked at the outer gate with the guard, as required. Just that scrawny servant with him."

Derg sighed. "Let him in. Nothing to be gained by putting him off."

Far swept into the room and greeted Derg warmly, as a friend. Derg replied with polite caution, keeping a good distance between them, staff or no staff.

The Dark Man piled his cloak into Oran's arms and settled himself comfortably, before getting to the point.

"You know I worry about Sive, alone in the wild."

"As do I," replied Derg tartly.

The sorcerer inclined his head sympathetically. "Of course. Still no word, I suppose?"

Derg shook his head. "I do not even know if she lives, let alone where she is."

"She lives," said Far, his hand brushing over his chest where the talisman lay hidden under the fine tunic. "I think you can count on that."

He trained his intense eyes on Derg. "I have news."

"Oh?" Derg tried to keep his breath even, his voice calm. Hard to imagine good news would ever come from this man.

"It was never my intention to cause such distress to your daughter. I thought, in time, she would reconsider my suit, but I see now I will never win her over. And I have met another woman, one who has kindled, and returns, my ardor." He smiled, his look of shy happiness almost convincing. "We are to marry in the spring."

"I see." What to make of such a statement? "May I know the name of your intended?" Derg asked carefully.

"Not just yet, I'm afraid." Far's smile became apologetic. "We have not yet made the announcement public, and of course we must speak to her family first."

"Of course." Had he found another with Sive's gift, Derg wondered. Or was this one of the Dark Man's ploys?

"I bring you this news for a reason." Far leaned forward in his seat, and Derg felt the force of the sorcerer's will beat against him. Finally, the point of this polite charade.

"If you have any way of contacting Sive, I hope you will tell her there is no reason for her to stay in this self-imposed exile. I have given her up and will trouble her no more."

Far stood up, all brisk haste. "Well, I have taken up enough of your time and have business of my own to see to. But I do regret deeply the hardship she must have suffered these long seasons, and I hope you will believe me that it is safe to bring her home."

"I would like nothing better," said Derg. "Sadly, I have no way to give her this message."

The sorcerer inclined his head gravely. "I see. Yet perhaps some chance will arise for you. I urge you to search for one." He flapped one hand to motion Derg, half-risen from his seat, back down. "Sit, sit," he said genially. "We will let ourselves out."

Derg sank back into his seat. His man found him there much later, lost in thought, the Solstice games forgotten.

DERG WOKE THAT night to a hand over his mouth, and perhaps the strangest words an assailant ever uttered to his victim: "Please don't hurt me, sir!"

His eyes flew open. A lamp guttered on the table, enough to make out the sorcerer's serving boy's face hovering above him, strained and urgent.

"Please stay quiet, sir. I mean no harm." The words were a strangled whisper.

Derg nodded, noticed his hands wrapped about the boy's neck, and slowly removed them.

Oran gasped a quick breath, his thanks coming on the outrush of air.

Derg sat up in his bed and waited while his heart slowed from its gallop and his brain caught up.

"What is this about?"

"Sir, I...I know something that might help your daughter."

Another trick? Derg considered the scrawny youth. He seemed scared to death, and not of Derg.

"And why would you wish to help my daughter?"

Oran winced and made a quick damping motion with his hands to quiet Derg. "Please, sir, I can't risk waking your man or anyone else. If my master finds out what I've done..." He glanced around the empty room, looking as if he might lose his nerve and take flight, and then visibly pulled himself together.

"Your daughter did me a kindness once," he said. "Not many do. If I can do the same for her, I will."

Derg knew that if Far Doirche had ordered Oran to come and present this story, he would be bound to do so. But would a man like Far even think of gratitude as a motivation? Would Oran speak with such feeling if he were under an enchantment? Derg threw out a fishing line.

"Far Doirche already explained to me that he no longer desires Sive and—" He was cut off by Oran's head shaking nearly off its stem.

"No, sir, you mustn't believe that! He wants her still. He's just hoping you'll bring her back within his grasp!"

Derg nodded grimly. The lad was honest in that regard at least. "Well then?"

"I might know another way," said Oran. "I heard Sive's sister Daireann talking and—"

"Daireann?" Derg's voice was sharp. "What has Daireann to do with this?"

"It's Daireann my master has been—"

Derg jumped up in anger. "He's after marrying *Daireann*?"

Oran's face twisted in distress. "Please, sir, please be quiet. If I'm caught…"

"I'm sorry, boy." Derg forced himself to sit back down and speak calmly. "It won't happen again."

"Well, I think he's just flattering her, sir, if you understand me, in hopes she will lead him to Sive. He sets me to, well, to spy on her, in case she mentions Sive's location. And what she said is that if Sive went to stay in Finn mac Cumhail's dun, she would be safe there."

"How would Daireann know such a thing?" Derg tried to summon all the lore and news he had heard of this Finn. Some relation to Lugh, wasn't he? And his dun just over on the Hill of Almhuin, though to hear tell he was rarely at home, traveling as he did all over the country.

"I gather she went wooing him once," said Oran. "And she cursed him or some such thing when he refused her, and he said if he were in his own dun no curse would touch him, because the hand of Lugh protected it."

As Derg pondered these words, excitement rose within him, as though Lugh's own light had kindled deep in his own chest. Lugh, beloved of the sun, could not be harmed by any dark creature or spell. And if Finn did indeed enjoy his favor...He would go to Lugh of the Long Hand and confirm what Daireann said. And if it were true, he would search all of Eire, search until the world's end, to find his daughter.

"Daireann said Finn would refuse any woman of the Sidhe," Oran said. "But I do not believe it. How could he refuse Sive, after all she has suffered?"

The boy's eyes were bright and indignant, his fears forgotten. Derg felt suddenly sure this was no ruse, but a genuine act of courage. He thanked Oran warmly and then said, "Is there any reward I can give you that your master will not discover?"

Oran shook his head doubtfully.

"What if we walk over to the kitchens, and at least get you something to eat on your way back to your room?"

The slightest hesitation, and then a very firm headshake. "I've taken too much time already. He is not a deep sleeper."

Sive Remembers

My father searched for me all winter, flying through every prov-ince of Eire, visiting the houses of kings and laborers, seeking word of a strangely spotted doe. And when at last he found me, in one of the lonely hidden valleys of the Mourne Mountains in the north, he was so relieved and so eager to tell me his news that he changed straightway.

And I ran from him. I did not know my own father. I saw only the two legs of a hunter, and bolted.

He had to hop and flutter before my nose, flying onto my back and annoying me in every possible way, before the memory of the magpie who had guarded my path as a child, and with it the memory of the man himself, awakened. It was long then since I had walked on two legs. It was as though my will and mind had frozen with the winter, and I had sunk into my animal skin and let it close over my head. If he had not found me, I might have remained submerged forever.

Once my mind woke up, I managed the change well enough. But time fleeted from us like the most timid deer, and we did not dare talk long. I could tell he worried that I would forget again, that the deer would take me before I could reach Finn's dun. But I would not forget. I had hope, and a plan, and the raking pain of denying my heart and leaving him. These were my reminders that I was a person, not a beast of the wilds, and I clung to them as I made my way down the coast until I found the river that would lead me to a string of three hills. One, back home, was my own hill of Sidhe Ochta Cleitigh. The middle one was just a hill. And the third was the Hill of Almhuin, winter headquarters of Finn mac Cumhail, head of the mighty Fianna.

TWELVE

She was a woman trapped in a deer's form, of that Finn had no doubt. Had he not seen it before? His own aunt Tuiren had been changed to a hound by a jealous woman of the Sidhe. Or perhaps she was like the puppies Tuiren had whelped at that time, his own Bran and Sceolan. They were born and would remain hounds, but with a human sensibility. Either way, the strange doe must be kept safe.

It would not be easy, he mused, with a deer. Bran and Sceolan were renowned for their prowess on the hunt, leaders of the pack that traveled with the Fianna. No man would think of harming them. But a deer would be in constant peril from men and dogs alike. Would he have to pen her up like a sheep?

His own two would do their best to protect her. What an extraordinary sight that had been. After the long day's chase he had climbed over that last ridge, wondering why his hounds had fallen silent, to find the little spotted doe nestled down in the bracken and Sceolan pressed snug against her, while Bran frisked about like a giddy pup.

Now Finn shrugged out of his tunic and breeches and slid under the heavy furs. It was cold, for he had put out the fires. Finn loved the early spring, despite the dampness and rain, despite the mud that could make the hunting trails nearly impassable. He loved the smell in the air, the heady sense of a world awakening, the way the lengthening days filled him with eager energy. And…he loved putting out the night fires, sleeping in clean air rather than a haze of peat smoke and waking with clear eyes and easy breath.

A good day, he thought, as he sank into sleep, a day filled with exertion and mystery. Had he ever run so far as after that doe? It was good to show the men his mettle now and then. But he was damned tired, no denying that. He would sleep well this night.

SIVE RESTED ON THE clean straw, soothed by the placid contentment of the horses sharing her little shelter. Her skin had finally stopped jumping at every yip from the restless dogs and shout from the men. The dogs could not reach her here. The human noises quieted as the men gathered in Finn's house. Sive's heart gave up its nervous race and settled into a steady rhythm; her legs rested gratefully on the earth. As the sun sank from the sky, Sive felt the blessing of a night without fear. The dark was peaceful, not threatening. She would sleep a bit, until the night was deep and silent.

She had never encountered hunters as determined as Finn's men. It had been a long, hard run—much harder than she had expected—to lose them. And as her father had predicted, Finn and his dogs did not drop out of the race, but stayed on her heels until the others were far behind.

She was at the point of exhaustion herself, otherwise she might never have found the courage to turn and stand. Finn's dogs were fierce and eager, their voices roaring through her head, and the deer in her was certain they would tear her apart.

"But *how* will they know me?" she had asked her father, but he had only shrugged helplessly.

"I cannot know for certain that they will. Manannan thinks that it is probable, for like recognizes like. It is a risk you must decide to take—or not."

For nearly three years she had been exiled, not only from the comforts and company of the hearth but from her own true nature. If she remained a deer much longer, there would be no returning. Steeling herself, she overrode the instinct that commanded her to run—to run until her heart burst in its cage or her legs collapsed beneath her. For a moment she just stood, trembling with fatigue and fear, head down, lathered flanks heaving. The hounds' voices swelled behind her.

Turning, she folded her legs beneath her and lay down on the grass. As the hounds scrambled over the rise and bore down upon her, she closed her eyes. She thought of the little fawn who had brought about her first change. It would be her neck, not his, that felt the ripping grip of teeth.

But it was not teeth, but Bran's hot breath in her face and his dripping tongue washing her muzzle, that she felt. And she opened her eyes to a new life.

HER FIRST SIGHT OF FINN had made her heart quail. Backlit in the late afternoon sun, he was a featureless dark outline of a man. Huge, he seemed, so tall and powerfully built. Even if they had not been shadowed, Sive's deer eyes could not make much sense out of human features. But she made herself gaze directly at him, pressing back the deer and willing her true self to speak to him through her animal eyes.

At first he did not move or speak. Sceolan pressed reassuringly against her. Bran gamboled about, sometimes scooting over to Finn and back. Still the great man stood silent. Sive held her breath. If he rushed at her, it would be all she could do not to bolt.

He did not rush or even take a step. In a voice softer than she had ever heard from a mortal man, he spoke to her. She did not need to know the words. She understood.

Slowly, Sive gathered her limbs and stood. The first hesitant step was the hardest. Once she started, she did not doubt her way. She followed the kind voice until she stood at Finn's side.

Quiet as ever, his voice changed quality as wonder crept into it. His hand eased out toward her, just a few inches, and stopped. Sive stretched out her muzzle and laid it into his rough palm.

"Will you come home with me?" Finn asked. The dogs were already leading the way. Finn turned to follow. And Sive followed Finn.

FINN STIRRED IN HIS BED. What had awakened him? The soft noise repeated itself, and his eyes flew open, heart lurching into an alarmed gallop. Then his reason woke up: the dogs at his feet were silent and untroubled. In fact, he could feel a tail thumping in welcome against his shin. This was no enemy creeping, sword in hand, to Finn's bedchamber. Brave enemy indeed, to enter a house where half the Fianna sheltered!

Sitting up, he peered across the small chamber at the shadowy figure in the entranceway. A single candle cast a tiny wavering light that showed little more than the hand holding it.

"Who is it?"

The figure came closer, holding the candlestick higher so that he could see.

She moved as though she were weightless, her feet barely denting the earth. Her gown shimmered over a body as graceful as a young willow. And her face...Finn had never laid eyes on a face so lovely, nor so troubled and full of entreaty.

"My lord."

She did not seem to know what else to say. Finn rose and took her hand, and sat her down on the end of his bed. The dogs edged over to lie close beside her, and she seemed to take comfort in stroking their great heads. Finn took the candle from her and used it to light his lamps, and then he pulled a spare blanket from his chest to drape over her shoulders.

He sat down across from her.

"You are the deer."

She nodded with relief. "They told me you were wise." Her voice like the low flute, making him yearn for it to continue. She offered a fleeting tremulous smile, and Finn's heart lurched painfully. "I couldn't think how to say that part to a mortal. It is three winters I have been wandering Eire in the body of a deer, sleeping out in the weather and eating…" Her voice trailed off, and Finn saw tears glistening in her eyes. He wanted to kiss those tears away, to lift the sorrow from her lovely eyes and make them dance with joy.

But first he must help her to tell her tale.

"How did this happen to you, my lady?"

"Sive." She blinked back the tears and straightened. "My name is Sive."

The story took a long time to tell, and when it was done, Finn knew he would do anything for this woman. He understood now why the poets spoke of love as an enchantment, for he had fallen under Sive's spell and had no wish to be freed of it.

Sive Remembers

I used to wonder at the women I heard of, women of the Sidhe, who gave their love to mortal men. Our own men, any number of them, are more handsome, more gracious, more accomplished. What would draw a woman to a son of the Gael?

That was before Finn looked at me. Has any man of the Sidhe ever looked at a woman that way? It is a look of wonder, adoration nearly, mingled with such naked, yearning desire…

But it was not Finn's desire that brought me to his bed that night. Yes, I slept with him. Not, as the Dark Man assumed, in payment for his protection. That was given freely. He did not hesitate for one moment when I told him my plight, but said only, "You are welcome here for as long as you wish to stay, and will be safe as long as I draw breath to defend you."

No, it was the urging of my own heart that led me to him. He was a handsome man, strong, open-handed and kind. His eyes told me that I was his most precious dream. And I was lonely, lonely near to madness. The weight of it, the crushing, utter exile that I carried without rest—I longed to put it down.

Finn opened his heart and his arms to me. And I laid down my loneliness and came home to him.

THIRTEEN

It was a joyful reunion, sure enough. Derg had never really felt right in his skin since he and his wife had parted, and he could not pretend to be unhappy at Grian's return. He lingered in that happiness through most of the bright afternoon before allowing his fears to intrude.

"You mustn't stay here, Grian. You know it's not safe for you. What if Far Doirche decides you are easier prey than poor Sive?"

She shot him a sly smile. "Oh, I think it will be safe enough now. My father has finally tired of my moping and is sending messengers to the Dark Man as we speak, to inform him what will happen should he so much as waggle his hazel rod in my direction."

At last. Would the Dark Man risk the direct enmity of Manannan? He must know the other old ones would join with their brother against him. Derg's heart lifted. The sorcerer was too cautious for that. He would not bring it to head-on war against such powerful enemies.

"And Sive? Does he give the same protection to his granddaughter?"

Her face fell. "I'm sorry, husband. I tried, countless times I tried. It is like trying to soften rock." She shook her head, avoiding his gaze. "He says he did not approve our match; therefore, he has no responsibility for its issue."

Issue. Derg's mouth tightened at the cold word, a word to match precisely the cold correctness of Manannan's reasoning.

"In that case," he said, not bothering to mask the anger that seeped into his voice, "perhaps he should look to the protection of his *approved* grandchild."

"Daireann? Why do you say that?" asked Grian sharply.

Daireann was her daughter, Derg reminded himself, as beloved as Sive. He should not have spoken so carelessly. He softened his manner, though there was no softening the words.

"Far Doirche has set his hooks into her and landed her in his net. He says they are to be married."

Now Grian was on her feet, the soft bed and warm embrace forgotten. She paced, indignant, incredulous, flinging out questions and looking ready to scratch out the eyes of the next person in her path.

"What does he want with her, for the love of Danu? And how could she be so stupid? And where is Bodb!

Is she not under his roof?" She turned, finally, and faced him head-on. "What is he doing, Derg? Why Daireann?"

"I think," he said slowly, trying to steady her by example, "that he is hoping she will somehow lead him to Sive. Which," he added, "she could inadvertently do."

Grian's puzzled look reminded him she knew nothing of Sive's new hope, and he shook his head apologetically. "I'll explain that part later. Right now, let's decide what to do about this match."

"There's nothing to decide," Grian said briskly. "I'm returning to Underwave, as soon as I've eaten, to tell my father. He'll send messages to Bobd, who will listen to him better than to me."

"I'll travel with you," said Derg. He opened the door of their chamber and called their attendants. He wondered if Grian's women had even finished unpacking. Perhaps Grian would take pity on them and allow them to remain behind this time. He and Grian would travel faster with just a couple of guards.

SIVE STEPPED FROM the house into the silky air of late spring. You could get drunk just from the smell on the breeze, she thought, gazing down the slope of the Hill of Almhuin to the green waves of land beyond.

The hill itself was carpeted in bluebells, pools and rivers of deepest blue flowing through the forest. Finn had walked with her there yesterday while she gathered armfuls of them, three of his men flanking them at a distance with swords at the ready. The bluebells didn't last though, here in the mortal lands. The flowers adorning her chamber were already starting to droop.

Dear Finn. He had done everything he could to make her happy in his home—and she was. She was. Only it was the confinement that was hard. She had always loved to roam the woods, and nearly three years of being unable to escape them had, it seemed, failed to destroy that love. In weather like this—surely no spring day in Tir na nOg could be more lovely—she longed to open the gate of the great wall that surrounded Finn's dun and simply walk, alone, unguarded and uncaring.

It could not be, and she knew it. Perhaps Finn would suggest a walk later—a short walk, too short for the Dark Man to take her bearing. But she would not pester him for it. She had overheard more than one muttered comment from his men, after an evening's drinking when they were louder than they imagined. They could not fathom why, after two months' marriage, he still played the homebody, more interested in listening to her songs with his head in her lap than getting on with the season's hunts. The time would come when she would have to gently urge him to take up his duties as the leader of the Fianna—but not quite yet. She had waited a long time herself to find such a love.

Meantime she had the back garden behind the cook-house. The cook's daughter kept it, for food and potherbs rather than beauty, but all young growing things are beautiful, and Sive found pleasure in the quiet promise of life springing from the dark soil. The peas were high and flowering already, she noticed, twining and thrusting their pale green stems round the sticks set in for them to climb, tiny pea pods emerging from the spent blossoms.

Sive found her favorite corner: the herb garden, where the smells of bergamot and lavender and sage all mixed on the breeze. Finn had set out a bench for her there, and she settled into it now and tipped her face to the sun.

She sat forward again before her back muscles had time to relax against the bench. Something had caught her eye, a flash of white and black winging down from the sky to perch on the wattle fence.

Sive shaded her eyes, hoping against hope that *this* magpie would be the one. She had watched for her father these long weeks, wondering why he did not come to check on her. But there was something purposeful in this one's flight that—yes—here he came, winging down to the herb garden and landing on her bench.

"Is it you, then?" she asked, and in the time it took to say it, he was there, sitting big as life in front of her and for once no need to hold back or hurry.

When they were done with their laughing and crying, and he had apologized for her long wait (saying only, and rather mysteriously, that he was delayed by "complications at home"), Derg cast his eyes around the grounds and said, "I would have expected something grander for a man of such repute."

Sive shrugged. "It is grand enough for these parts." She bristled a little inside, for it was *her* home he criticized, though he did not know it.

Derg glanced at her quickly, perhaps sensing the offence. "Well, he has taken you in, and that is the grandest thing of all," he said quietly. "I hope I will be able to express my gratitude in person."

"I'm sure he would love to meet you." Sive made as if to rise, but Derg reached out a hand to stop her.

"In a while, daughter. It is long since we could talk at our leisure. I find I am loath to share your company, even with the man who has made it possible."

Sive dimpled at him, the glint in her eye very like to her mother's.

"You will like him, Father. I do."

"Any man who...," Derg began. Then he looked more closely at his daughter's expression.

"Sive. Are you saying...are you telling me that you love him?"

She nodded, her smile open and luminous now. "I am. I do. And he feels the same. We were married nearly two moons ago."

And only a few days after their first meeting. No wonder Derg looked so stunned! Well, if it was a rash act, then he and Grian had only themselves to blame, having started the family habit, so to speak.

"Oh, my dear." To Sive's surprise Derg's voice held not the concern she expected, or even gladness, but a kind of quiet sorrow. "You have married a mortal?"

She nodded. "He is a good man, Da. He is well worthy of it."

"But this." Derg waved his hand to encompass Finn's round house—little more than a huge whitewashed mud and wattle hut—the clutch of dark guest houses, stables and outbuildings scattered around it, the garden where they sat, a drear and graceless shadow of the lush, colorful gardens of home. "You will bind yourself to this? When the day comes that Far Doirche is defeated and you are set free, will you not long for your own lands and people?"

"When." Sive's voice was flat and hard. "You should be after saying *if*. It's many seasons I have been longing for my own lands and people already, and no return in sight. Finn could be dead in the grave by the time the Dark Man is defeated. In the meantime, what prettier place would you have me choose?"

She should not have spoken like that, out of her anger. He did not understand how differently she saw things now. How could he? And now he thought she had wed Finn out of despair.

She laid her long fingers on Derg's arm. "I am sorry, Da. That was just prickleburr talk." An expression from her childhood, one Derg used from time to time to soften Grian's sharp tongue. "It is no fault of yours that the Dark Man still hunts me, and it is because of you that I am safe here. But because of Finn, I am more than safe—I am happy.

"I know," she said, holding up her hand to forestall his reply. "I know how this place looks to you. And your eyes see true. My clothes are plainly woven, the food is coarse, the house dim and clumsy. But Da"—and now she held his eye, needing him to feel the truth of her words—"none it matters. I am warm and sheltered and well-fed, and now I understand the value of these things. And I am loved."

There was no need to say more. There were, after all, few men of the Sidhe who loved with a devotion as steady as Derg's.

Sive Remembers

Did I not yearn for my homeland? On a clear day I could stand on Finn's lookout and see the very hill that, in another world, was crowned with the beautiful buildings of Sidhe Ochta Cleitigh. On a summer's night, I could almost imagine I saw the glow of a hundred candles and lamps, and heard sweet music drifting across the still air.

Yet most of the time that world was far away, like a dream that fades upon waking. This world—Finn's world—was so solid, so immediate. Even when it was unpleasant, it demanded my full attention.

And then there was my Finn. How I loved the man! It was a marvel and a sorrow to me, that a man so full of life could be destined to die. He had a great booming laugh and a smile that spread beyond his face into the very air. His hands were big enough to circle right around my waist and gentle enough, despite their calluses, to make me sigh with pleasure. And somehow his mind was the same—capable of large impulses and subtle distinctions, of childlike wonder and wisdom beyond his short life's experience.

I did not lower myself to marry Finn, whatever my father thought. I was proud to be his wife, and prouder still when I learned that I carried his child. I was happy. And so I cast thoughts of the Dark Man from my mind. I would not allow his shadow to cloud my happiness.

FOURTEEN

Daireann was white-faced with shock.

"What do you mean, leave off? We are to be married!"

Far shook his head. His eyes were tender and sad.

"No longer, I fear. Your father and grandfather have set themselves against us."

"Oh, and what of it?" She tossed her hair back with a sniff. "They were against my mother's match as well, but she made her own decision and is the happier for it. Do we need their approval to live our lives?"

"Daireann, stop." The voice, still gentle, held a hint of the cold iron will at its core. "I will not show our great ones such disrespect as to defy their wishes for their family. And I will not cut you off from your own people."

Daireann flung herself at him, clinging to the blue silk of his tunic, stroking his chest, trying desperately to spark in him the love she thought they shared.

"I don't care about that! I don't care about *them!* Far, I love you and you love me. The rest doesn't matter."

But he was prying her away from him, holding her back with a stiff, locked arm. His expression cold, the iron unsheathed.

"Leave me." The words were flung at her like a blade, and she flinched as if they could actually cut. The green eyes bored into her, held her like a vice. "I do not love you. I will not marry you. You will leave my sight and never approach me again, or I will take up my rod and compel you."

She backed away slowly. Now she saw the sorcerer that others feared, and yes, she was afraid, so afraid her legs drained of their strength and could hardly hold her. But she was also, more than ever, attracted to his power. She had been his chosen one, his love, and now he cast her off as carelessly as a cloak.

Suddenly she was released from his gaze. The handsome face became dreamy and faraway. His hand clutched at the pendant at his neck.

"She stirs," he murmured. "She reveals herself at last." His lips curled into a small, private smile. "And where have you ended up, my pretty one?"

Finally Daireann understood. Her fear was subsumed in her rising anger. The blood rose hot in her face, her legs grew strong again with rage.

"It's *her!*" She fairly spat the word out. "This has all been about her! You never gave her up at all."

The green eyes locked on hers once more. His smile was cruel and careless. "And yet you proved to be of little use. A waste of time, in fact."

Red with humiliation, Daireann could hardly wait to be rid of the sight of him. But she had never been one to give up the last word.

"Go to her then," she snarled. "Spend your life chasing after your precious Sive, for all it is to me." She turned, trying mightily to sweep grandly out of the room when everything in her wanted to run.

And as she went through the door, talking more to herself than to Far, she said, "I hope she *has* gone to Finn. Better him than you."

THE HOUNDS' STEADY baying changed to a sharp, urgent barking. Good—they had found it at last. Finn and his men broke into a jog, hurrying after the dogs' call. A lone wolf was no easy prey. This one, lacking a pack to hunt with, had come out of the wilds to rampage through the herds instead. Judging by the string of sheep and calves it had killed, it was no sickly, feeble outcast.

It would be well dark before they returned home. The dark came earlier now, and with it the cold. It would be Samhain soon, the night the spirits walked abroad and the barriers between Eire and Tir na nOg dissolved.

Finn felt a hard knot tighten in his belly at the thought. On that night, he would not leave Sive's side, nor the gates of his dun.

He was anxious to get back to her now. Thinking logically, she was even less likely to venture beyond the gates at night than on a fine sunlit day, but fears are not always logical. Finn did not like to be away after nightfall.

He did not, in fact, like to be away from her at all, and it was only her urging that had persuaded him to rejoin his men on their hunts. He would not roam the country with them, as before, but took his grudging place with those who remained behind to hunt the bogs and hills surrounding the Hill of Almhuin.

Finn's thoughts were interrupted as they came upon the hounds, ringed around a bristling gray wolf. It was a scene of furious noise and vicious threat, the dogs all hackles and teeth, the quarry red-eyed and desperate. As they approached, it broke and rushed at the smallest of the dogs. Finn knew the other men felt the same jolt of nerves as he did—up close, the sheer power of a full-grown wolf was stunning. His heart swelled with pride as Bran and Sceolan flew in, throwing themselves like projectiles at the wolf's flank and dragging it back. Brave hearts both, they were, and as dear to him as any two-legged friend.

Finn took little pleasure in the rest, though he did not allow himself to lose focus. Caoilte got the kill, but a hunt is a group effort. Just as on a battlefield, a moment's inattention can get a man, or his comrade, killed. It was not until the long hike home that Finn allowed his impatience to surface.

Finn had not needed Sive to point out that the men were restless and uneasy that he stayed at home. He saw it well enough, and it annoyed him. Were they not grown men, well able to manage a hunt on their own? Did they, the most skilled and hardened fighters in Eire, need him to be their nursemaid, when he had a more important task before him?

Of course, they did not have the knowledge he had. To their eyes, he was simply captivated by his little love nest.

They should know and trust him better. For it was given Finn to see beyond what normal eyes could see, to sense truths that were veiled from other men. And he knew the Dark Man watched his wife. Finn felt the man's brooding presence, lurking beyond his gate. The Dark Man watched and waited.

Finn fell back to relieve the man carrying the front end of the pole that sagged under the wolf's weight. He hoisted it onto his back, taking the brunt of the burden, and quickened the pace. He needed to get home.

DID IT NEVER STOP raining in this infernal land? Far hunched his shoulders in irritation against the rivulets that wormed their way between his cloak and the back of his neck, and shrank farther under the yew that was supposed to be sheltering him.

He grew weary of this chase. At first the surprising stubbornness shown by that timid slip of a girl had amused, even pleased him. Nothing wrong with a challenge, and she was, after all, a prize worth some effort. Now, as the end drew near at last, he resented every additional hour he had to spend here. But if she thought he could be deterred, she would soon discover her error. Each day that she eluded him made it more imperative that he succeed. It was personal now, his need to prevail a greater spur than the interesting weapon she would become for him. He would *not* be thwarted by a mere girl.

His chance would come. He had only to keep a grip on his patience a while longer. He would not risk an encounter with Finn mac Cumhail, though it pained him to give way to a mere mortal. The blond giant was clearly more than he appeared, for he had once withstood the magic of another great sorcerer of the Sidhe, a man by the name of Aillen, and killed him.

But Finn could not stay locked in his white hovel forever. One day he would leave, and when he did, Far would be ready.

Meantime, there were preparations to take care of. Far pulled his cloak tighter and continued to follow the pathway Finn and Sive had taken just that morning, his sharp eyes examining every outthrust branch and muddy footprint. The dogs were easy. The dirty creatures left gobbets of gray fur behind wherever they went. But men shed too. A thick yellow hair, a drop of blood on a bramble thorn. Even a clump of fibers from Finn's cloak would serve, if he had worn it often enough.

Far continued on his methodical path. No one, not even the magpie winging over the trees to Finn's white dun, noticed his presence.

PART II
THE DARK MAN

FIFTEEN

Finn had been gone seven days. That wasn't long for the journey to the coast and a battle, Sive told herself—a day longer than he had estimated, but nowhere near long enough to assume "anything untoward" had happened.

Anything untoward. That was how Fergal, the man charged with the dun's safety in Finn's absence, had put it. Very delicate phrasing for a man pitted and scarred by battles past, but Sive knew what the words stood for.

Finn dead on the strand, the lapping tide drawing out a red wash of his blood. Finn spitted by an enemy spear or hacked by a sword, his breath coughing out frothy and red, his belly black and festering, his leg green and reeking of poison. Finn and his men outnumbered and trapped, fighting a hopeless battle with ever-dwindling strength.

She must stop. Sive made to leap up from bed, was checked by the new weight of her belly and settled for sitting up slowly. A sweet burden. She would not be leaping anywhere for another couple of months. The child within her rolled and stretched, and she cupped her hand over the tiny foot-shaped bump that appeared under her ribs, smiling as it pushed against her and then pulled back, disappearing into the secret world within her.

She would not rush to the lookout to stare down the road leading east—not yet. She would rise, and dress, and eat, and chat with the women, and attempt to make garments soft enough for a baby out of the rough wool and linen made by the daughters of the Gael. And when she could not stand it a moment longer, *then* she would go to the lookout and watch.

THEY HAD BEEN LUCKY to have a peaceful winter, Sive reflected. The wind up on the high lookout was raw, but she could smell the spring in it. Spring was in the brighter shade of green in the fields rolling down toward the sea and the busy, boasting calls of the birds. The trees were still bare, but it would not be long.

Life had grown quieter at Finn's dun after Samhain, when the coming and going of the summer season died down and the men—all but Finn's own company—dispersed to their own border forts and posts to keep watch over the land.

Sive had worried when Finn said he would not attend the high king's feast at Samhain.

"Do you not serve King Cormac?" she asked.

"Aye, though he chooses to forget it on occasion." Finn's voice was mild, but Sive sensed an old anger.

"What do you mean?" she asked.

Finn shrugged. "When the country is quiet, he resents our wages. He sees only the provisions and pay, but not the returns."

"And when there is war?"

A quick, bright smile. "Then we are the King's most loyal, most valued, most dearly loved Fianna."

"And he will expect you on Samhain, to confirm that loyalty, will he not?"

Another shrug. "This year, I have a more pressing duty, which is to see you safe through the night. I will send my best men, Goll and Caoilte, and the King must be content with that."

Whether he was or was not content, Sive did not hear, but she was glad to have Finn by her side through the long dark of Samhain. The protection over Finn's dun held though, and the Dark Man did not enter.

And then the winter settled over them. Men cooped up too long can grow restive and quarrelsome, but Finn kept his men busy with training and challenges and patrols. At night the feasting hall was raucous and high-spirited. Sive could hear them sometimes long after she had retired to the white house to sleep. Yet there was poetry and music too, and Sive enjoyed singing with Finn's musicians. The food grew worse as the months passed, but the music improved steadily.

The call had come on the last new moon. Invasion on the coast, by the men of the Northlands over the sea.

"It's not far," Finn had told her. "An easy day and a half to the bay of the River Liffey, and we'll still be plenty fresh for the fight."

He turned to her then, his face grave. "Promise me you will not leave the walls of the dun until I return, however long that may be."

"I won't. You know I won't. Don't worry, Finn. I am safe here."

"You are my heart," he murmured, and his kisses chased the Dark Man from her thoughts.

It was not until he was taking his leave that the new fear struck at her.

"Finn..." She clutched at his powerful arm. For the first time she fully realized he might not return. A mortal man: how easily he could be killed, how terribly fragile the skin that shielded him. Men of the Sidhe died in battle, occasionally. But unless they were killed instantly, there were few wounds that could not be healed. Here there were no magic waters, no mending spells, no silver hands. There was terrible pain, injuries that left men crippled and broken, and death. Death as common as nettles.

"Be careful," she said, unable to find any words to match the enormity of her vision.

He saw it. The blue eyes crinkled in gentle amusement.

"Never fear, girl. It is not my time to die, not yet." He placed his index finger under her chin and tilted her head so she met his gaze directly. "It is given me to see things other men do not. I will be back here, alive and well."

She nodded mutely, not trusting herself to speak again without tears.

All these men's wives and lovers, she thought, as she watched the long line of men striding through the gates and down the road, disappearing into the wooded slopes of the hill and then visible again, now just small dark shapes, snaking across the outlying fields. All of them saying goodbye, over and over, not knowing if it's for the last time. How do they bear it?

A SMALL HAND plucked at her cloak. "Ma says won't you come inside now, Lady Sive, and warm up by the fire?" Earnest gray eyes peered up from within a frizzy halo of hair.

She *was* chilled. Sive had a new appreciation for the rough deerhide that had protected her through three Irish winters, now that she had only her own soft skin and woven cloaks against the weather. She smiled at the girl.

"Thank you, dearie. That sounds like a good idea."

A haze of peat smoke hung in the air of the house and stung her eyes, but the fire's red glow and blooming heat made up for it. Searc had pulled a chair up close to the hearth, and she settled Sive into it now, fussing over her as though she were a fragile invalid.

"You must be careful, m'lady, not to overtax yourself or give the baby a chill."

Sive smiled. She had been in Eire long enough to see that the household women hardly slowed down at all until the very end of their pregnancies. She had seen a hugely pregnant woman heaving tuns of ale into the storeroom, and another cutting peat bricks with her man on a windy day spattered with rain. But they treated Sive like an exotic flower that might droop and drop its petals at any moment.

"Thank you," she said as Searc tucked a blanket around her knees and pressed a warm mug of sweet mead into her hands. "I'm fine, really."

Goll's wife came by soon after and was easily persuaded to join Sive at the fire. She set about entertaining Sive with stories of their men's adventures and exploits, peppered with her own dry commentary. That was one thing the same in both worlds, Sive had been glad to learn—the mixture of admiration, irony and bawdy humor with which women talked about their men. It was from Ana she learned what had actually happened between Daireann and Finn, how Daireann had made him curse and abuse his men so vilely that all but Caoilte had left him in disgust, and how poor Caoilte had spent the day running all over the country chasing down the Fianna and persuading them to return, until at last Finn came back to himself and could apologize and explain. Ana laughed till the tears ran down her broad cheeks, repeating the outrageous things Finn had yelled out under Daireann's spell, and that gave Sive courage to broach a new subject.

"You have been a good friend to me here. Can I ask you something?"

Ana was a down-to-earth, plainspoken woman. She would settle the uncertainty that had been stopping Sive's tongue.

"None of the women ever ask about my life before I came to Finn. I'm not sure if that's because I should not talk about it, or because you don't want to pry?"

Ana sighed. "It's both, my dear. We want to know it all—of course we do. Sometimes I'm so curious about you that I think my head will burst open if I don't ask!"

"Then why don't you? I don't mind telling."

Ana shook her head, her full lips pressing together as if holding in a crowd of questions. "It's not for ordinary people to know about the Secret Lands," she said darkly. "It's dangerous to know too much. Our men find their way there now and again, and it's few that ever return. It's only the druids and suchlike who can survive so much magic."

Sive considered this, wondering what to say. Surely talking about Tir na nOg was not the same as going there. Besides, the men who didn't return were as likely to have fallen in love and been permitted to stay as to have met a bad end.

She was saved a reply by Ana's hand on her arm. "There is one thing though," she said, her eyes glinting with excitement. "Do you still have the dress you came in? They say it was more beautiful than anything a queen would wear here."

"I'll get it," said Sive. "No, for pity's sake, it's only a few steps."

She was halfway to her chamber when she heard the yelling outside.

"What? What is it?"

Searc was at the doorway, listening. She turned to her mistress, her plain face shining.

"It's the Dord Fiann! They've heard the horn of the Fianna, Lady. The men are returning!"

Sive snatched the blanket from her chair as she passed by and threw it around her shoulders as she hurried to the gate.

THE SWEET NOTES of the horn floated on the air, announcing his homecoming. He smiled in anticipation. By the time he came within sight of the gates, she would be watching for him.

The two dogs ranged about him as he strode up the hill. Hard to look the returning hero at this time of year, he reflected wryly, when you had to skirt around patches of sucking mud on the path and mince across slippery crusts of half-melted snow.

The track emerged from the wooded slopes of the Hill of Almhuin into the cleared area surrounding the dun, and a cheer went up from the walls. He waved, scanning for a willowy figure with hair like red gold. There she was— waving with both arms, her hair a bright banner in the sun. He had forgotten how beautiful that hair was.

A little farther. Would they wonder why he came alone, without the Fianna? Sive would not. She would think he had run ahead in his eagerness to see her. And so he had.

He could see her clearly now, arguing, it seemed, with the great fellow towering beside her. He had his paw laid over her arm, and she pulled against it.

He smiled. She would come to him. He waved again, only for her this time, and then flung his arms wide in a gesture that could only mean one thing.

Sive disappeared from view, and in moments the gate opened and she came flying out to him. Her belly sailed before as she ran, heaving with each step like a ship in a swell.

A bolt of rage took him by surprise. What was it to him who the vixen lay with? Yet the sight of that belly, filled with the get of the interfering mortal who had somehow stood between him and his prize—that was maddening.

Her steps faltered. Losing her breath, no doubt, from that load she carried. Still, he must be more careful. He had come too close to giving himself away. He smiled, pulling the great form of Finn mac Cumhail more firmly over his own face, pouring his concentration into a demeanor of loving delight.

She continued toward him. But even as he reached behind to snatch up his rod and raise it high, she gave a cry and veered awkwardly, sliding in the slick mud.

He could not believe how instant her change was. Before he could bring down the rod over her shoulders, before her slithering turn could become a fall, she was a blur of red-brown fur, leaping away on four slim legs.

Far's rage was no longer contained, but roared from his throat in a torrent. The illusion melted away, and he stood revealed, no longer the coarse warrior of the Gaels but the green-eyed, subtle sorcerer with the monstrous will.

She would not escape, not this time. The mud bound her; the child's weight dragged at her. The dogs—not Bran and Sceolan, but Far's own bound creatures—flung themselves at her throat, and she could not shake free of them.

It was the work of an instant to tighten the looped cord around her neck and drag her back into the woods.

Finn's men were pouring out of the gate, pounding after them. Far's lips curled in contempt. Mortals. What did they imagine—that he would stand here and cross swords with them?

Fog roiled up from the earth, oozed from the leaves of the trees, seeped out of their trunks. The air darkened to the blackness of deep night, though the sky above remained bright with sunshine. Strange sounds and cries filled the woods, seeming to come first from one direction, then from another. The frantic men blundered this way and that, fighting their way blindly through the woods, drawn by the illusion of a barking dog or a woman's cries to one false trail after another.

They would find no one. Far was gone, and Sive with him. She would never lay eyes on Finn again.

SHAPESHIFTER

Finn Remembers

For years I searched for her. Through all of Eire, every mountain and hidden valley, year after year, I searched. I felt her loss through my waking and my sleeping, as though some evil magic had cut the heart from my chest, and I still living on without it. But the Dark Man had taken her to a place I could not follow. The gates of the Sidhe were closed to me.

SIXTEEN

*S*ive Remembers

Finn was farseeing, but he could not see everything. He did not see that I would never hold him, or admire his blue eyes, or sing him to sleep again.

When I understood how the Dark Man had tricked me, I was sure I would die of grief. I longed for it. But whatever all those tales of great love say, it is not so easy to die of a broken heart. The body betrays the heart and keeps it beating.

Then one day the baby squirmed and stretched in my belly, and I wished for a mother's hands to soothe and cradle him. My mind, which had been doing its best to fade away altogether, jolted awake as I realized the dangers of the birth to come. I still had one thing to live for: my baby. Finn's baby.

SIVE STOOD WITH hooves splayed, head down, as the contraction gripped her, clenched hard, and released. They were coming faster now. Time she was under cover.

Sive did not know what had prompted Far Doirche to agree to her desperate offer. Pressed against the far wall of the shed he had shut her in, ready to turn if he so much as waved a toe over the threshold of the doorway, she had bargained for her baby's life. "Allow me to bear my child, and raise him to the age of fostering and send him to his father," she had begged, "and then I will take my woman's shape and submit to your rod, and go with you."

"You are joking, I suppose," he had said, and behind his smile the anger had been a white heat that licked at her like a flame. "Why should I not kill the child the day it is born?"

"Because then you will have no way to compel me, and I will be a deer to the end of my days before I bend to your will." The words so brave, while she had to clasp her hands behind her back to hide their trembling. It was only her singer's training keeping her voice from betraying her. "Besides," she had added, letting go of the defiance and softening her tone, "what is seven years to a man such as yourself? It will pass in a few nights' sleep, with long centuries ahead for you to savor all your victories."

She had been sure he would see the weakness in her argument. But Far, who could work an illusion but hadn't the fellow-feeling for true shapeshifting, knew nothing of its laws. And the law was this: she must have the baby in her true form, or he would be born a deer, and like the wolfhounds Bran and Sceolan, be doomed to remain a beast forever.

Another pain flared, bit deep and eased away. But she was close now. When the contraction ended, Sive turned off the little track and began to make her way through the trees to the shelter she had prepared.

It wasn't much—just a hollow scraped under the splayed roots of a fallen tree, lined with bracken and screened with piled-up brush. A beast's nest, it was, not nearly as comfortable as the cave Far had provided in this oddly spacious prison—a seemingly open woodland walled by such thickly woven spells that it might as well have been an island in the midst of a vast sea. Sive could not break through its invisible walls, nor had she ever seen so much as a moth pass through from the other side.

Sive was not about to give birth in that cave, whatever the Dark Man had promised. He would sense her change, and what promise in any world would stop him from preying on her weakness? No, she must be hidden. There was nowhere she could go in Far's "garden," as he called it, where he would not find her. She knew that. She hoped only to slow him down by making him search. To change at the last possible moment, bear her baby, and return to four legs before he arrived.

She sank onto her forelegs at the mouth of the shelter, then eased onto her side as a fierce pain radiated through her belly. She would stay and labor here, in the dappled sun—warmth for comfort, light for courage. When the time came, it wouldn't take her a moment to scramble down into the scrape and pull a few branches across the opening.

SHE NAMED HIM OISIN—little deer—but to Sive's great relief that was the only part of him that spoke of deerness. He was a big, strong, eager baby boy, with his father's blond hair and open smile, and the deep, clear jewel-like eyes of her own people. He was her only joy and a constant low-grade terror, for babies are ever in need of care that only a woman with soft hands and clever fingers and a soothing voice can give, and though she longed to lose herself in these tender encounters, she could not. Every moment spent in woman's form left her open to the Dark Man, and she never changed without ensuring she had a clear view, or a solid wall, in every direction. She cleared the area all around the mouth of the cave and did her mothering deep inside, so he could not take her unawares.

At least she was adequately provisioned. The Dark Man did not intend for her to die in her captivity. There was little in the way of comfort, but there was fire and food and occasional fineries intended, she supposed, to tempt her away from the exile she had chosen. When the Dark Man came with these things, she would huddle against the back wall of the cave with Oisin and take her deer form, always keeping the baby behind her so that Far hardly got a look at him. Sometimes, when he came, he would speak softly to her, hold out a fine dress or a jeweled pin enticingly, but she would not respond. As time passed, his tone was more often threatening and angry than pleasant, but it was all the same to her. She cowered against the wall and prayed he would not harm Oisin.

She never slept in her own shape but always as a deer, curled protectively about her baby, so he was able to snuggle into her warm flank and find her milk easily.

And so Oisin survived and grew into a sturdy toddler with blond-white curls and a clear, piping voice that could already follow his mother's tune.

Sive Remembers

My Oisin. He comes to me in my dreams some nights, and I awaken in the rustling blackness before dawn with the imprint of his sturdy little body pressed against me, the feel of his mouth greedy on my breast, the heat and weight of his head and the sweet baby smell of him...And then comes the loss. The long, long years since I have seen his dear smile or heard the music of his laughter. Are you alive, my son, and running with the Fianna? Or did Far betray us and leave you, so young and helpless, to die?

Oh, on those mornings, if I woke to the music of the hounds, I think I would give myself to them, for it does not seem possible to go on. Instead I run. I lose myself in blind flight and run until my hide lathers and my flanks tremble, until the last drop of my strength is spent. I run until thought is replaced by simple animal need, and I forget.

THE YEARS DRIFTED PAST as they do in the Undying Lands, like leaves resting lightly on a river's surface, seemingly still but soon carried out of sight by the strong invisible current. So it was for Oisin, who grew overnight, it seemed to Sive, into a lively boy who knew every ivied oak and rabbit run of their wooded pen. But Sive had never been so aware of time's march, each fleeting year a step closer to the day the Dark Man would claim his due.

He tried when Oisin was five, sending Oran to the cave as messenger since she would not take her own form in Far's presence. "He will come tomorrow at first light," Oran reported. "He says you are to be in your proper form, ready to go with him."

Oran, a boy no longer but a bony young man with wide brown eyes, did not try to disguise his sorrow as he recited his message. "I am sorry," he told her. "I hoped you would escape him."

As had she. Her bargain had been necessary to protect her son, a mother's instinct that could not be denied, however disastrous the consequences. And those consequences had seemed so far away. Surely Far would be overcome before they could come to pass, would show his hand once too often and set the Old Ones finally against him.

Now Sive saw it would not happen. He was careful; he had kept his plans and his prize hidden from sight. But he would not have her yet.

Sive bristled at Oran, a show of defiance for his master's benefit. "Your master has mistaken the age of weaning for that of fostering," she declared, though Oisin had been weaned a year and more. "Since when do we send babies of five summers from their mothers? You may tell the Dark Man I will give him up in his seventh year and not before."

Her bluff had worked—once. But the following spring Oran was back, with a more ominous message. "My master says some boys are fostered at six. And he will not wait longer. Be ready at dawn tomorrow."

Sive refused again, and at dawn, when Far did not return, she breathed a sigh of relief. Another year gained, or so it seemed.

But the Dark Man had come. Hidden in the woods, wrapped in the shadow-spell that faded him to a dim hint of a man, he waited. He waited until Sive had cautiously released her golden-haired boy from her tight embrace. He waited through their morning meal, until Sive stopped peering fearfully into the woods at every snapping twig and rustling leaf. He waited until the sun's wheel had carried it to the highest point of the sky, until Sive relaxed her guard and sent the boy for water. And as Oisin walked carefully back from the brook, both arms wrapped about a heavy earthenware pot, Far Doirche stepped out from behind the blackthorn and scooped the boy into his arms.

Oisin nearly got away. His mother had taught him well, and keeping hold of him was like trying to pick up a nest of weasels. He twisted, he bit, he kicked out viciously with a child's version of his father's thick-muscled thighs, and in the end Far held nothing but a fistful of blond hair which he did not doubt the boy would gladly tear from his own head if it meant escape. When he felt Far's iron blade bite against his neck, though, he had the sense to grow still.

Sive had come flying from the cave at Oisin's first screech and stood before them now, wild-eyed and agonized.

"There will be no more games." Far snugged the blade closer and pressed, enough to make the boy wince and bite his lips. Eyes round and blue in a white, scared face. He gave Sive time to imagine the next steps and then continued calmly, "You will come to me now, or I will kill your child in front of you. Choose."

Oisin Remembers

"You must send him to his father," my mother begged. She was frantic, weeping, and I was numb with terror, though she had tried to prepare me for this day. She clawed at the Dark Man's cloak in desperation. "You will send him? You promised me!" Her voice shrill with fear, the bleak knowledge before her that she had no power to hold him to anything at all.

"I have already said I would," he said absently, like a husband half-listening to a scolding wife. His concentration was all on the words and gestures that wove his invisible web across the entrance to our cave. He had bound me carelessly and tossed me in the far corner of the cave, and I wrestled frantically with the knots, trying to free myself before he was finished.

And then he dragged her off.

The ropes fell away and I hurled myself into that barrier again and again, trying with all my might to follow. I howled and screamed and threw myself against the unseen wall until my voice was a husk and my face smeared with blood.

My mother kept twisting herself to see me, yet she did not fight to escape him. He had laid his hazel rod upon her, and she could not but obey him. But she cried out my name, screamed it as though it were ripped from her heart by a clawed hand, her beautiful face a mask of loss.

Soon she was gone from my sight, and the only sound in the woods my own hoarse cries. I battered myself against the Dark Man's wall until exhaustion swallowed me up like an ocean wave. One minute I cried and fought; the next, darkness took me and I, too, was gone.

SEVENTEEN

S ive couldn't say how long the journey took to Far's
house or what path brought them to his door. She
saw nothing but her last glimpse of Oisin crying after her,
fighting to break through the spell that held him fast. The
thought of her little son locked in that cave, the swelling
fear that the Dark Man would simply leave him there to
starve, shrilled inside her like a silent scream.

The house was hidden deep in a darkly wooded valley,
as unwelcoming a dwelling as Sive had ever seen. Far strode
inside, dragging her behind him and pushed her to the floor.

"I have much to do," he said. "You will not leave this
house until my return."

Sive hardly heard him. Hours of weeping and begging
while stumbling over rough country had left her gasping
and choking on her own breath. But she had to try again.

She lowered her head to heave in a lungful or air and managed to find some voice.

"My son. Please…"

It was as though she had not spoken. Far did not pause or look at her as he strode to the door.

Before he left he looked back.

"You will not kill yourself. And you will remain in your woman's body at all times."

And so Sive was left, alone and unguarded, in a house she could not escape. She slumped on the floor where he had tossed her, and the silence settled around her.

She had made a catastrophic mistake. "Why do you say *in thrall?*" she had asked her father, so many years before. Now, too late, she understood. She was trapped. Anything she might do to defy or escape him, even unto death itself, he had only to forbid.

She was beyond weeping. The unseen sun sank toward the horizon, the forest darkened to twilight, and still she sat, unmoving and silent. There was no need for torch or candle. No light would brighten the pit she had fallen into.

SHE JUMPED AND SHRANK back when the door banged open, but it was not the Dark Man. Oran shouldered in, a hamper filled with peat bricks in one hand and a bucket of water in the other. He stopped when he saw the woman on the floor. Her features were hard to make out in the dim room, but he knew who it was.

"So he has you at last," he said sadly. "I am sorry."

Sive was grateful he did not say more but continued on to the back of the house and presumably the kitchen.

She could hear him moving about, and soon tendrils of scent—first peat fire, then cooking—floated into the front room. And then his worn boots stood before her, and he spoke to her again.

"I've made dinner. It's not—well, I don't imagine it's what *you* would call dinner. Just oatmeal and turnips; it's all he allows. But there's food if you're hungry."

Sive shook her head.

"You might as well eat, you know." The words were blunt, but Oran's tone was gentle. "If he sees you're starving yourself, he'll just order you to eat."

"Not tonight." Her voice not much more than a whisper.

Oran nodded and returned to his meal, but now Sive was faced with a new problem. She hadn't relieved herself since midmorning. Talking to Oran and smelling the food had made her aware of it, and now it was a clamouring need.

Reluctantly, she got up and followed the smell of turnip until she found Oran. He looked up from his bowl.

"Change your mind?"

"No, not that. Oran—" She was embarrassed to ask, but there was no getting round it. "Where is the latrine?"

He pointed with his spoon to a door, smaller than the one at the front, at the far end of the room.

"Out there. Take the path to the right. Not much more than a pit, I'm afraid."

She couldn't open the door. She walked up to it, unbarred it, and could not make herself push.

"Oran, I can't…"

"Trouble with the door?" He jumped up. "It sticks sometimes. Here." He put his shoulder against it and gave it a good shove, and almost fell as it opened without resistance. "There, now." He held it wide and waved her through.

She couldn't do it. Could not take one step over the threshold, could not seem to make her legs understand what was required. She strained to pass any part of her body through the opening until the sweat stood out on her forehead—and failed.

And the memory crashed in: *You will not leave this house.*

"I can't," she said, slumping against the frame in defeat. "He forbade me to leave."

IN THE DEEP BLACK silence of the night, the door opened again. This time, it was the Dark Man. Sive knew him by the tendril of cold air that snaked along the floor ahead of him and licked over her shoulders, freezing the base of her neck. She knew what that cold air was: it was the breath of evil.

But he strode past as though she were a piece of furniture, and it was Oran who crept in at first light, silently coaxing back the fire. He put a cautionary finger before his lips when he saw her watching and then waving vaguely toward the far end of the house, put his hands under his head and closed his eyes.

Sive nodded her understanding. She was in no hurry to wake Oran's master either.

My master. The thought came unbidden, unwanted. *He is my master now.*

ONE LONG, ANXIOUS DAY stretched into another, and Far Doirche showed no interest at all in the prize he had waited so long to capture. At Oran's timid suggestion, Sive was given a pallet and blanket against the west wall of the house, and permission to go out to the latrine. Apart from that, the Dark Man spoke to her only once, in a tone of complete indifference that did not hide his harsh message.

"I'm told it is very unpleasant to eat under duress," he said, biting with fierce gusto into a roasted rock pigeon. Though his tone was contemplative, his voice carried easily across the great open room that made up most of the house. Oran, who appeared to be Far's only servant, flicked his eyes over to Sive where she crouched on her pallet.

"More ale, Oran! Pay attention!" Far snapped. Oran winced and bent hurriedly to pour from the heavy pot in his arms.

Sive thought about it, imagining her hands pushing food into her mouth, her throat swallowing mechanically. The next day she took the fried oat cakes Oran offered and made herself eat them.

Far Doirche, it seemed, was rarely at home. Sive could well understand why he would prefer to stay elsewhere.

His was the meanest house she had ever seen in Tir na nOg. Finn's house in the mortal lands was far better appointed. As far as she could tell, the house had only three rooms: the great room in front—all but empty, with neither feast tables nor sleeping nooks for guests—Far's private chamber, and the kitchen.

When he *was* home, Far spent hours hidden away in what Oran called, in a nervous undertone, "The House of Magic."

"What is that?" asked Sive.

"It's where he keeps all his materials for enchantment, where he makes his spells."

"Where is it?" There were no buildings that she had seen within view of the back door or the latrine.

Oran shook his head. "We are not permitted to know."

"You've never been there?"

The young man's pale features grew drawn, the eyes dark with memory. The lips pulled tight, barely allowing his whispered reply to pass.

"Once."

Sive was silent, sorry to have stirred up whatever evil memory Oran was reliving. But when he came to himself, she blurted out the question she could no longer keep to herself.

"Oran, what is he up to? He hunted me for so long, and now that he has me, he pays me no mind. Which I would have go on till the end of time," she hurried to add, "but it makes no sense. Has he given up on using me?"

"Ah, no." Oran shook his head. "He never gives up, Sive. Never. But he is careful, a schemer. I do not know just what he is doing, but he will be laying his plans, setting all in place. When he is ready, he will put you to work."

IGNORED BY HER CAPTOR and confined to his dark house, Sive could not escape her own thoughts. She thought of Finn and their short season of happiness together. She thought of her years in the wild as a deer and wished bitterly that she had remained a beast and never tried to regain her life as a woman. And she thought, always— the way a song can play through your mind, insistent as a heartbeat, whatever else you are doing—about Oisin. The memory of her little boy battering himself against Far's barrier haunted her.

Oran was a quiet friend, coaxing her to eat, finding a head cushion for her thin pallet, bringing her a sprig of bluebells or the deep red valerian that grew in the cracks of the stone well. He talked lightly of the weather and the thrushes nesting under the eaves—and just once, of Oisin.

"I know how you fear for your son," he said. Sive lowered her eyes. Just hearing it said aloud made her tremble.

"I do not know what the master did to him," Oran continued. "And if I ever have the chance, I will go to the cave and see if he is there." He cut off her rush of thanks. "But Sive, what I wanted to tell you is this: I do not think he left your boy there. Why else did he set out so quickly after bringing you here? And"—he groped for words—"it may be I have imagined this, but…there is something about Oisin, and his father as well. Something that disturbs him. I have never thought this about him before, but I almost think he does not dare to kill your boy."

EIGHTEEN

After a two-day absence, the Dark Man blew through the house like the cold gale that scours the western coast. "You!" he snapped as he swept past Sive. "On your feet."

Sive's legs were pushing her upright before her mind had confirmed that she was the "you" in question.

"ORAN!" The bellow blasted through the empty room and brought Oran running in from his chores, ax still in hand.

"Master?" The young man's chest was heaving, and Sive wondered uneasily just how far away he could have been and still heard Far Doirche through the heavy walls of the house. It was as though the Dark Man had yelled directly into his ear.

"Baths, Oran. Two of them. The girl first."

Oran ducked his head and trotted away. Seconds later, Sive heard the back door bang.

A bath. Despite her grief, Sive's heart gave a little flare of eagerness at the thought. It guttered out soon enough; Far's clipped orders saw to that.

"I have clothes for you. After you have washed, choose a dress suitable for traveling. You can put on a more elegant gown when we arrive. You will have to do your own hair for now."

The green eyes flicked over her. "What are you waiting for? The bath is in the kitchen."

Sive scuttled past him to the kitchen. She prayed he would not follow her.

SIVE HAD NOT THOUGHT such gloomy lands existed in Tir na nOg. Two days' travel through dense woods and bog under a dark sky had brought them to this house, modest by her old standards and absolutely splendid compared to her master's home.

"Like me, Donal has few neighbors," Far remarked as they approached the house. "It has been easy to cultivate his friendship, and he is eager to host a celebration of our wedding."

He reined in his horse, and Sive's mount stopped without any direction from her. It had been like that for the entire journey: the horse carried her like a load of grain, and completely ignored her attempts to direct it. Oran, she noticed, did not even bother to hold his reins.

Far Doirche turned his horse to face her. "Did I mention we are married?" His smile was mischievous and tender. "I imagine there will be plenty of teasing and toasts for my lovely new bride." The smile vanished, and the green eyes bored into her. "You will play the part of the happy bride. You will say and do nothing to suggest you are held against your will. You will not mention your singing or my powers…" The instructions continued, boxing her into a narrower and narrower space until there was nowhere to step but along the Dark Man's path.

DONAL'S HOSPITALITY was so warm and genuine that it broke Sive's heart. A minor chieftain in a remote corner of the country had cause to welcome any allies he could get, but their welcome went far beyond the requirements of politics.

"My friend!" he exclaimed, clapping Far in a warm embrace. "I am delighted you have joined us. And this"—he offered Sive his hand and bowed low over it—"this must be your beautiful lady. Welcome, my dear, and know that we are at your service. If there is anything at all you need for your comfort, you have only to say the word."

Sive was murmuring her thanks when Donal's wife Marga bustled in. More introductions and kind words, and then Marga said, "But where is the Lady Sive's retinue? Have you not brought your women?"

Far Doirche's smile was a perfect picture of embarrassed apology. "We intended to, of course, but didn't Sive's maid fall on her ankle the night before we left? It is not broken, we think, but very swollen and painful. Sive, who is very tenderhearted, as you will learn"—and here his green eyes fell fondly upon her—"insisted her second lady stay to care for her injured sister."

This brought gasps of sympathy and indulgent chuckles, along with the immediate offer of a woman to attend Sive throughout her stay.

"That won't be necessary," said Far Doirche briskly. "We'll manage very well with Oran, here, if you could just lend the Lady Sive someone to help with her hair and toilet?"

Unlike the handful of other guests, they were given a room of their own, whether in deference to their recent marriage or to Far's esteemed status, Sive didn't know. Far had been holding Sive so tight against his body that she feared he would take her the minute they were alone, but he cast her from him as soon as the door closed. Striding to the storage chest, he fished out a blanket and tossed it at her.

"I don't imagine you will sleep well sharing a bed with me," he said. "And we must have you looking your best. Perhaps you and Oran can draw lots to see who gets the pallet by the hearth, and who the floor."

DINNER WAS A QUIET AFFAIR. Apparently most guests were due to arrive on the morrow, when the feasting would begin in earnest.

"If you are asked to sing tonight, you will sing prettily, no more. You will give no hint of your voice's power," Far Doirche had commanded. It was a relief to know that nothing would happen yet; still Sive knew that the Dark Man was only biding his time.

It was hideous, eating and talking with these people and being unable to warn them of what was to come.

"Sive, you are lovely, but so thin!" exclaimed Marga. "Far Doirche, you must feed her up."

Marga's own figure was rather solid, Sive observed, a shape more common among mortals than her own people. A great wave of longing swept over her—for Finn, for her house on the Hill of Almhuin, for all the friends and servants who had welcomed her. For her child.

"Lady Sive? Are you well?" Marga was peering at her, round blue eyes under brows furrowed with concern.

Sive felt the corners of her mouth lift—a death grin, it felt like, rather than a true smile, but apparently it looked real enough, for Lady Marga's face lit up in relieved response.

"Of course," Sive heard herself saying. "I'm so sorry— I was just cloud-walking. A little tired from the journey, I suppose."

"I quite understand," said Marga. "Here—try some of this." She pressed a silver goblet into Sive's hand. "My own recipe, very reviving. Oh, and have some honey babies."

She winked, leaned in and whispered, "You must build up your strength, for when you have a green-eyed honey baby of your own."

The thought made Sive weak with nausea. Yet she felt her cheeks dimple and blush, and her hand reached for the rich sweet and popped it into her mouth.

THE NEXT EVENING some twenty guests filled Donal's cramped feasting hall. A small gathering, not many more than would assemble for any ordinary meal back in Sidhe Ochta Cleitigh, but as much care had been put into this event as for any great feast. The room glowed with the soft light of many candles, fixed into elaborate wrought-iron chandeliers suspended from the ceiling. The candlelight was reflected in the gold and silver plates, the metal inlay on the ceiling, the jewels of the women and the gleaming armbands and torcs of the men. The guests were richly arrayed in colorful silks, flowing sleeves, intricate hairstyles, sweeping cloaks.

Sive's dread grew with each bite of their elegant dinner. How many times, in the bogs and gloomy forests, had she yearned to be in just such a place, surrounded by the light-hearted chatter and bright, beautiful company of a feast night? And now she walked among her people as their betrayer, her return an evil mockery of her dreams. In her head she screamed out a warning to them all, cried to them to flee, to stuff their ears, to cast her out. And still she ate and smiled and nodded and chattered with the rest.

Soon enough the moment came. Donal had invited a harpist to entertain his company, but that would not forestall what was to come. It was common for guests to take a turn, and sure enough, as the last sweet chord of the harp's latest tune lingered in the air, Lady Marga turned to Sive and said, "You have a lovely voice, as we learned last night. Would you favor our guests with a song?"

Sive Remembers

Even as I felt the pretence of a modest smile jerk at the corners of my mouth and felt my head nodding assent, I was determined to defy him. Had I no will of my own? I was not like Oran, taken by the Dark Man as a young boy, beaten and terrified into submission until he could conceive of no alternative. I was strong from my years in the wild. My son was dead or gone—free, either way, of Far Doirche's grasp. There was nothing binding me to life, and I would let him crush my brains before I sang to these people.

A great hand scooped me from my seat and propelled me toward to the front of the hall. I did not fight it. My hope was to take Far Doirche by surprise, to feign compliance but keep going, right through the small doorway to the side which the harpist had come through. The harpist smiled his welcome and I nodded in return. But my mind was all on the doorway behind him, and on hardening myself against the Dark Man's will.

I had not taken two steps past him when the pain stabbed into my head—skewers behind my eyes, fire burning through my skull. This was not the simple barrier that had kept me from the latrine—it was the Dark Man's fury that fell upon me, his rage at being crossed.

I fell to my knees, clutching my head. My face was slippery with sweat and tears. A terrible noise ripped the air—my own tortured screams. It was as though he was flaying me from within. My mind scrambled after something, anything, to hold on to. Finn swam into blurry focus—my Finn, so courageous and proud—but the Dark Man cast him out with a lash of fire.

Then came Oisin, my beautiful shining boy, and in my anguished sight it seemed to me he stood untouched by Far Doirche's wrath and called to me. I clung to that image—clung with all my strength—until with a roar Far sent a curtain of fire leaping up between us, and I lost my senses.

When I opened my eyes I was standing beside the harpist, looking out over a roomful of smiling, relaxed people. The harpist was running his fingers experimentally over a tune, his eyebrow raised in inquiry. I ran my hand over my hair, amazed to find my forehead dry, my braids perfectly in place. I heard my own calm reply. I understood then that what I had just experienced had passed between myself and the Dark Man alone. No one had heard me cry out or seen me writhe on the ground. No one had noticed anything in the least amiss. There was that moment of stillness that alerts an attentive audience that the performers are about to begin, and then a cascade of plucked notes rippled over the harp and ended in my opening chord.

And I sang. With no more will than a child's doll, I sang until every man and woman in the room was overcome with *peaceful drowsiness, and slept. I sang while Far Doirche went out to the place where he had hidden his hazel rod and brought it into his friend's feasting hall and touched it to each sleeping head. Though it seemed to me that I wept and pleaded, cursed and shouted, the voice that poured out of me was warm and sweet as honey.*

The next day Donal's guests joked about how strong Marga's mead must be, for none could quite remember my singing or even taking themselves to bed. And each time Far Doirche spoke, I saw the deep luster of their eyes become dull and they would hasten to do his bidding.

"A promising trial run," he said as we left Donal's house. But I was filled with a horror so deep the ocean itself could not drown it.

I had done wrong to bargain with the Dark Man. It was folly to put my child's life above the hundreds he would now enslave. But what mother could count any price too high for her own child? Even now, the only hope remaining to me was that Oisin lived.

NINETEEN

They had hardly returned when Far bustled away again, to Sive's intense relief. He left Oran with a long list of chores, some so strange and sinister-sounding—replenish the crows, grind more bone—that Sive did not dare ask their meaning.

"I'm off after greener pastures," Far announced cheerfully, as though the entire household shared his enthusiasm.

Sive had been in numb despair through the long, wet ride home, unable to face any thought at all. Now, with Far Doirche's paralyzing presence gone, her courage returned.

There had to be a way out, if only she could find it. Long into the night she paced the house, or sat slumped against the wall, knees drawn up and head cradled in her arms. She tried to recall every comment she had ever heard about the

Dark Man. She reviewed everything she had learned about him during her long captivity—his pride, his secrecy, his indifference to women. Was there a weakness she might make use of? She tried to summon her father's cleverness, to look at her plight with the bright, curious eyes of a magpie. She confronted head-on the question that had haunted her these past years—why had nobody found her? Was her father even searching for her anymore? He would have been barred from entering their secret valley, she realized, just as she and Oisin had been barred from leaving it. For all she knew, the Dark Man had been able to shield it from sight entirely. But now—would word not get out that Far Doirche had taken a wife? Would Derg take up the search again? It was a long string of ifs to hang her hope on—too long. If word of her existence reached Derg, if he found her, if he presented Manannan and the other Old Ones with proof of Far Doirche's treachery, and if they stood against him...how many people, by then, would be under the Dark Man's spell?

She could not wait for her father, or anyone else. It was her voice. She must find a way to still it.

It was late, the deep silent black of night, when Oran clumped through the back door. In the weak light of his lamp, Sive saw how his shoulders slumped with fatigue. Yet when he saw her awake, he came and sat beside her, setting down the lamp so it flickered and danced before them.

"I went to the cave," he announced. "The barrier is down. Your son is not there."

Sive was silent. She could find no words for the gratitude welling up in her heart. It did not mean Oisin was alive—she knew that well. But it was enough for her to believe he was.

She rested her hand on Oran's arm and squeezed in silent thanks. She thought again about the long oppression he had endured, and the risks he had taken to help her, and realized she had misjudged his strength.

"Oran," she murmured. "I must never sing for him again." He nodded gravely. He had seen as well as she where the Dark Man was headed.

"Yet wherever I turn, I can find no escape." She peered at his pale face. "Can you help me think?"

The light flared, catching the deep shadows under his eyes, his gaunt cheeks. He looked exhausted.

"You're tired," she said. "I should have realized. You've already made that long journey for me. Perhaps tomorrow—"

Now it was his hand on her arm, staying her. "Sometimes fatigue brings odd ideas that escape a person in daylight. Tell me what you have tried already."

Sive summarized her day's long, unhappy wandering.

"So," Oran concluded, "you cannot kill yourself because it is forbidden. You cannot leave this place without permission. You cannot change to your deer form. By the time word reaches your father or Manannan that Far has you, he will have an army of men at his disposal. And I will add that, in all the years of your captivity, there has been no word that I've heard of Finn setting foot in Tir na nOg, which makes me think the Dark Man has managed to bar its doors against him."

He sighed, running his hand through his dark hair and over his face. But Sive had an idea, a good one.

"Oran!" She paused, unsure of how to put it, and then said it directly, remembering that he had not flinched away from talk of suicide. "*You* could kill me."

He shook his head. "Forbidden." And then smiled sadly. "Also, I am not at all sure that I could bring myself to do it."

Oran stood up, stretched and yawned. "I'm going to fall asleep at your feet. Let's brew this overnight, and perhaps our dreams will whisper an answer."

SIVE HAD NO DREAMS. She lay stiff on her pallet all night, her mind racing over the same dead-end roads, her belly in turmoil. By dawn, she was as drawn and pale as Oran.

Oran skipped breakfast to catch up on his chores, refusing to allow Sive to help. She was limited, in any case, to the house and the path to the latrine. And so, again, she roamed the close confines of Far Doirche's dark walls, wrestling with her fate. Only as the sun neared the top of the sky did she find some relief in building up the kitchen fire and filling the hanging pot with water to boil barley.

By the time Oran returned the house smelled of grains and cabbage and the tiny wild onions she had found growing in a fragrant patch beside the path.

He was pleased, she could tell. And hungry. He was halfway through his bowl before he came up for air.

"I haven't forgotten last night," he said. "The only new thing I've thought of is that there are sometimes holes in his commands."

"Holes?"

Oran's brow furrowed as he tried to explain. "We are bound to follow his words exactly, but not necessarily his intention. Sometimes that leaves an opening he didn't see."

Sive went over the commands he had given her so far. She didn't see any openings. She didn't even really understand what Oran meant. "I can't...was there a time it happened to you?"

Oran nodded. "That's how I was able to tell your father about Finn mac Cumhail. Far Doirche told me to inform him if Daireann said where you were. He didn't tell me to inform him if she said where you *might go*, and so I was able to hide that from him. Not that it did much good, in the end."

He went back to his bowl, scraping the last drops from the bottom, and then pushed himself up from the table. "I'm sorry, Sive, it's not much. I'll keep thinking."

The door was almost closed behind him when he thrust it open again and poked his head back inside.

"How exactly did he say it?"

"Say what?" Far had said many things, she thought impatiently, and then regretted it. Oran had no need to help her at all.

"When he forbade you to turn to a deer. What were his exact words?"

Sive thought back. It had been her first day in this accursed house. She was exhausted, muddy, thrumming with fear for Oisin. And the Dark Man had paid her no more mind than a sack of potatoes, except to throw his commands over his shoulder as he left.

"You will not kill yourself. And you will remain in your woman's body at all times." She repeated the words back to Oran, who nodded thoughtfully.

"In your woman's body."

"Oran, what?" He had hold of something, she could tell.

He cocked his head to one side. "Is the head necessarily included with the body, I wonder? And if not, could you turn just your head, and leave your body as it is?"

Sive Remembers

All afternoon I tried. To change one part only—it is impossibly hard. And the Dark Man's prohibition was clamped over my body, hard as tree bark. My muscles trembled with the strain, the sweat ran down my brow and arms and between my breasts, my mind strained to escape the bonds of his spell. But I could not find the division between body and head.

Last light found me slumped with exhaustion and despair, too tired even for tears. It was Oran who coaxed me to eat a bit and shooed me into bed. "You look near to collapse," he said bluntly. "You must rest."

"But if he returns—," I protested.

"If he returns, you will try again after he leaves," said Oran. "Or"—he hesitated—"is it his spell that prevents you?"

I shook my head. "I don't think so. My head does feel different. I just can't do it."

"So, it is a difficult feat. Yet you try to achieve it when you are half-dead from exhaustion." He laid a hand on my shoulder gingerly, as if he feared overstepping himself, and spoke gently. "If it is possible to do this thing, you will need all your strength for it. Sleep now."

I woke in the waiting dark before dawn with a dream, or a dreamed memory, so vividly upon me I felt it in my very bones. I had dreamed of the time my father came to me and made me turn back my change to keep me hidden from Far Doirche. I had felt again the jarring pain of it, how the smooth flow became fragmented, each part at odds with the other, as the streaming transformation slowed and reversed.

I lay quiet for a while, reliving every step of that memory. I knew now that different parts of my body could be affected separately from the others, and I remembered how it felt.

I held on to that feeling as I prepared myself. This time, I knew I would succeed.

TWENTY

It was a glorious early summer afternoon. Far didn't usually pay much heed to the weather, but it was hard to ignore a day matched so perfectly to his mood. The warmth that quickened the blood, the rain-washed luster of the leaves, the heady smell of growth. It was a day full of the promise of a new year. His year.

For he stood at the very brink of his dream. All the study, the craft, the long seasons of patience and scheming had borne fruit at last. Not that he would lose patience now. No, stealth and care were in his nature. No fear that he would throw away the prize in a rash grab for power. Bit by bit at first, nibbling away quietly at the lesser chieftains and remote sidhes, until there was a secret army, his for the summoning.

And then quickly, before there was time to organize resistance, the big festivals. Sive would sing, and they would all fall—all but the few great ones who were too strong for such tricks. Those, he would make peace with…for now.

The father must not hear of her. In fact, Far would be wise to dispose of the father as soon as possible.

But first he would play with his new toy one more time. His target was perfect—a proper sidhe this time, not some little hole like Donal's, but so swallowed up by dreary bogland that few outsiders could be persuaded to visit. Funny how even Manannan's enchantment had done little to beautify the bog, Far mulled. He chuckled to himself. Doubtless it would seem lovelier when it was his.

He kicked his horse to a trot, anxious to get home and get on with his plans. It was a bone-jarring, unpleasant gait, but nothing could mar his good spirits today.

THE DAY WAS OLD when Far returned, though with the Solstice so close the sky was still bright and blue.

"Oran!" he yelled as he banged open the door and strode in.

Far swatted at his leggings, raising dust and the smell of horse and travel sweat. Sive's nostrils flared at the acrid scent.

"Oran, a bath! And a decent dinner!"

The back door creaked, and Oran scurried up, panting.

"Just in time, Oran," Far said smoothly. "I almost had to punish your inattentiveness."

"I'm sorry, master." Oran kept his eyes on the floor, waiting to be released to his duties.

"A nice haunch of something tonight, yes? And a very deep, very hot…" Far stopped. He took a long, silent look at Oran. Oran did not move, but Sive could smell the fear rising from him. The tension in the room grew dense as fog.

"OR-an?"

"Master?" The boy risked a single, nervous glance.

"What have you been up to?"

Oran swallowed. "I've been doing the chores you left, master." A truthful answer, but not the one Far sought.

"Look at me, Oran."

And she was discovered. Just before Oran's reluctant eyes met Far's, they darted, helplessly, to the dark corner where Sive huddled under the eaves. Fleeting as thought, but Far caught it.

He whirled on his heel and stared at the monstrous thing that was Sive, and it seemed to her that his eyes blazed into green flame when he saw what she had done.

THE DARK MAN'S rage was like molten fire, burning everything in its path. He screamed at Sive like a warrior taken by the battle rage. She was terrified he would kill Oran. He swung his fist into the side of Oran's head and dropped him like a stone. Then he set in to kicking him: stomach, back, face, anywhere. Sive closed her eyes against the anguish of it. How could she stand by while her friend suffered? She was so close to giving in, so close. But then the Dark Man stopped and turned from Oran as though he didn't even exist and narrowed his eyes at the fantastic creature before him. He was calm again, summoning his power.

"Change back to your woman's head," he commanded. But he could not command her head. He could not hold her deer eyes with his own green ones. Sive was already receding from his grasp. She had been a deer for so many years that, once changed, it did not take her long to distance herself from her own mind. She retreated into deerness, further and further away from the place where he could touch her.

"We'll see," he said then. "We'll see how long you will defy me." And he put a rope around her neck and dragged her out into a drafty shed and shut her up.

For days she was alone in the dark, starving, thirsting. She didn't care. She was ready to die. And with each day her woman's mind grew weaker, and the deer's stronger, until by the time he dragged open the slatted door and let the sunlight flood over her, she hardly understood his words.

On that day he bludgeoned Sive for long hours, with his magic, with his whip, and at the last with a branding iron. And when at last he understood that he could succeed only at making her bawl and writhe with pain, he snatched up his hot iron again and hurled it into the trees. And then he turned to Sive, very slowly, and she trembled for she was sure her death was at hand.

But he would not let her die. He extended his one finger toward her. Drew up one leg like a stork and closed one eye. The position of the curse-hurler.

"You wish to remain a deer," he said. "I grant your wish. Become a deer, and remain a deer, and live as a brute beast to the end of your days. I wish both men and wolves joy of the hunt."

Sive Remembers

So many feelings I have had about being a deer, since the day I first mastered the shapeshifter's skill.

At first I was in love with it, as delighted and glowing as though it were my first man. I loved the rush of triumph as my form streamed into another's, the wonder of a world discovered through scent and sound and obscure, unnamed instincts. The sheer pleasure in my own speed and power.

And then it became a prison. In the first years of my exile, I longed to escape, trapped in a life driven by hunger and fear and without the smallest comfort. I came to hate my rough pelt, my bony legs, the long outthrust snout that blocked all song or speech in my throat. There was nothing I wanted but to return to myself and to the light and warmth of my own kind.

No more. He thinks he has punished me? He has given me refuge. I allowed Sive to sink beneath these layers of hair and sinew and muscle and vanish into their depths. I buried my sorrows and regrets and strangled hopes. I set my only aim to be survival, my only desire a full stomach. I forgot my own name.

PART III
OISIN

TWENTY-ONE

The boy is naked, curled against the cold dawn wind that sweeps across the mountain's flat top. He shivers in his sleep, and his fingers grope against the ground as if searching for a lost blanket or companion. They close briefly around a tuft of wiry grass before tucking back in against his chest.

He is only young, small but sturdy, with long golden hair. When he awakens in the first slanting light of the rising sun, he sits slowly, as one still in a dream. His eyes—beautiful eyes, clear as deep water and blue as the spring bluebell—are unfocused and confused. As he takes in his surroundings, his chin begins to tremble. He has no idea where he is.

A sound, musical and savage, rises through the mist that hides the mountain's feet. He knows that sound. Hounds, on the hunt.

Oisin Remembers

I may be one of the mighty men of the Fianna now, and Finn mac Cumhail's son, but for all that I still have nightmares about the day I woke up on the great slouching mountain men call Ben Bulben. I thought the Dark Man had sent me to the desolate ends of the earth, a world empty of everything but cutting wind and seeping mist and a monstrous upheaval of rock. I was only six summers old and had never been out of my mother's sight. No army or battle since has matched the terror of that morning.

THE MOUNTAIN WAS a great looming ledge. Its head thrust up from the land, bare sides scored as though by a giant bear claw. The long tail sloped back more gently, though it was hardly the smooth grassland it appeared from a distance. Crisscrossed with deep ravines and unclimbable overhangs, Ben Bulben was tough-going from any point. Finn was, in fact, growing tired of hauling himself up and down its flanks.

Yet there was something about this hulk of a mountain, and not just the wild boar that hid in its cracks and gullies, that called to him. Two days ago he had perplexed his men by hiking right to the summit and walking the length of Ben Bulben's flat, wind-scoured top. Had it been lopped off by the Dagda's war club in a fit of rage, as some believed? Finn had his doubts. He had met some of the Sidhe—killed one, for that matter—and seen their magic too. He didn't think there were many with a swing *that* vast, magic club or no.

Now Finn shook the clouds from his head and concentrated on the chase. Boar hunts his men understood; it was the nearest hunting came to military training, an exercise in discipline and trust as well as skill. When a big boar broke cover, you needed to count on the comrades at your side.

Boar was Finn's quarry of choice for personal reasons too. He had finally, reluctantly, after earnest counseling from Caoilte and Lughaid and other wise friends, stopped searching for Sive. How many times had he quartered the island? In how many places and ways, when he had at last concluded she was not to be found in his own land, had he tried to get into hers? Yet despite his wisdom, his learning, his far-seeing, despite his kinship with Lugh and his bag of power which had once been Manannan's, he had not found a way.

He had given up that hunt. But he would never again in his lifetime join a deer hunt without fear that it would be Sive that was found and killed before he could intervene. Foolish, that fear. His men knew well to spare all spotted does. If Sive were hunted to her death, it would not be by the Fianna.

The hounds' steady baying shattered into a frenzy of barking. They had something. Finn heard an excited shout from one of the men, hollered back and forced his legs to climb the steep slope faster.

The dogs were in view, a ring of lunging, eager back ends on the far side of a shallow gorge. A deep bass growl rumbled beneath the chorus of barks. Only Finn's two wolf-hounds, his Bran and Sceolan, had such voices, growls that throbbed deep in your chest and carried beyond the racket of lesser dogs. He quickened his pace, picturing his beloved companions cornered and in danger.

His men were converging now, and they covered the last distance together, scrambling and sliding into a seam sliced into the mountain's side, shoving through the gorse-choked bottom and finally coming up, winded and sweat-streaked, behind the ring of hounds.

It was a sight he never expected to see: Bran and Sceolan faced off against their own fellows. Hackles up, lips drawn back from their great teeth, growls swelling from their throats like thunder—this was no play-fight or squabble over a bone. This was deadly menace.

It's Sive. The thought was instant and inescapable. What else would they be protecting? Finn's heart, already pounding with exertion, thudded into a painful, lurching gallop, and he began hauling dogs back by their collars, flinging them one after another back to the men.

"Call them off!" he roared. "Tie them!"

He heard Caoilte's voice behind him, repeating the order and urging the men to action. Bless the man. More than anyone, he knew the pain Finn had lived with these long years.

The dogs' clamor faded back, and the wolfhounds quieted, ears softening, tails gently waving.

"What have you found?" Finn, with hardly spit in his mouth to speak, rasped the words out. He tried to see beyond the two dogs but could make out only a dark wall of rock.

They sidled apart to make way for him as he stepped forward. He observed, as if watching another, that his legs were shaky with tension. His heart drummed in his ears and broke his vision into sharp, shattered glimpses.

There was a recess in the cliff wall, a little scooped-out cavity in the rock. And yes, there was a figure inside its shadowed shelter. Finn lurched forward.

Not Sive. He knew before he could really make out the features that it was not Sive. No grown woman was ever that small.

Finn squatted down and peered in at the seated figure in wonder. A child looked back at him, a naked, cross-legged child with long blond hair and eyes that...oh, those eyes! As blue as his own, they were not Finn's eyes, nor the eyes of any son of the Gael he had ever met. They shone like jewels and shimmered with the secret depths of a sun-kissed lake.

Finn's head swam with questions, but he settled on one: "How did you get here, lad?"

The boy—he could not be more than six or seven summers old—searched Finn's face without replying, and Finn began to wonder if he was simple or could not speak.

Then the corners of his mouth twitched into a shy smile, and Finn's hot skin puckered up in sudden gooseflesh. He knew that smile, had seen it the very first night he and Sive had met, and he had kissed its lovely corners more times than he could count. Then at last the child spoke.

"Find Finn."

The boy had the high, fluty voice of a child still, but Finn could hear the music in it. Tears started into his eyes as he opened his arms wide.

"You've found him, lad. I'm Finn. You're safe now. You're with your father, and you're safe."

TWENTY-TWO

For six years Oisin had lived in near silence, with only the sounds of the woods and his mother's voice. Apart from the occasional, dreaded appearance of the Dark Man, he had never seen another person.

Now he was plunged into the life of the Fianna, surrounded by loud, rough, boisterous men, many of whom had women to match. It's not that he was treated unkindly; rather the opposite. He was their darling, with every man vying to teach him a skill, impart a wise lesson or make him laugh, and the women cosseting and petting him whenever they could pry him away from the men.

It was exciting and terrifying at once, and in those first months there were times when he felt he might be crushed by it all. Then he would run away and hide, and the longing that came over him for his mother and their quiet little world squeezed his heart so painfully that he didn't see how he could go on. He wasn't brave enough or strong enough. Sometimes he wished he could become a deer himself and spend his life alone in the forest.

But Finn—his father—helped him. If he found Oisin huddled behind a storehouse or crying in the woods, he would lift him up and just hold him without talking. Sometimes Finn would take Oisin into his own chamber, build up the fire and leave him with Bran and Sceolan. Oisin would press himself into the flanks of one or the other, and the quiet, steady presence of the great gray dogs, nearly the size of a deer themselves, comforted him in a place talking could not touch.

Finn saved the talking for the times when his son was not overwhelmed by his new home. He wanted to know all Oisin could tell him about how they had lived and what had happened to his mother, though the telling made Finn groan and beat his chest in helpless anger and sorrow, and reduced Oisin to tears. Yet it was a comfort, too, to know there was another in the world who cared about his mother's fate.

Oisin had never slept in a bed, never seen a sword, never eaten meat (there was no deer meat for months at Almhuin, on Finn's orders). But he learned quickly, and by Samhain he had lost his shyness and dogged the footsteps of the Fianna as if he had been born among them.

It was a fine, brisk autumn day when the anger came over him. A day for a young boy to roam the country-side and be glad for the life rushing through him, it was, and Oisin had been doing just that. With Bran and Sceolan at his side, there was little harm could come to him, and Finn was happy to see him venture out on his own.

But something swept over him—perhaps guilt at his own happiness, or a sudden glimpse of what life could have been had his mother stayed safe within the walls—and before he knew it he was scrambling up through Finn's wooded hill, bursting through the gates with fire in his eyes and his small chest heaving with rage.

Finn was enjoying the weather too, propped against the wall of his house with his legs in the sun and his head in the shade of the thatch, "chewing his cud" as he called it after a hefty midday meal. Oisin rushed over, drew back his foot and kicked his father under the ribs with all his strength, then fell upon him with a flurry of fists.

Later he would realize he was lucky that Finn, startled out of sleep, hadn't thrown him across the yard or stuck him with his hunting knife. Instead the great man had lumbered to his feet, shucking him off like a stable fly, and held him at bay by the shoulders.

"Hold, lad, hold!" Finn peered at the red-faced, tear-stained fury of a boy, arms still windmilling the air between them. "What's this all about?"

"Why didn't you save her?" Oisin shrieked. "Why didn't you find her? She came to you for protection, you told me so, and you let him steal her!"

Finn's ruddy face darkened almost to purple and he abruptly let Oisin go, turning away with his own great hands

fisted into clubs. Oisin's rage drained out of him as quickly
as it had come, and he looked with sudden fear at his father.
He had gone too far, insulting the man who had saved his
life and called him son. He looked up at the angry tower of
Finn's rigid body and back down at the fists clenched at his
sides. It was too late for apology. Finn's punishment would
fall on him at any moment.

But Finn did not raise his fists, or even his voice, to
him. When he spoke, his voice was husky and cracked, and
Oisin realized with shock that it was tears, not anger, that
his father was choking back.

"Do you not think I tried, lad? Do you not think
I would spend my life, and gladly, for even the least glim-
mering hope of saving her?"

Oisin could not speak. He was confused, shamed by
his own actions. Of course he knew Finn had tried to find
Sive. Nearly everyone at Almhuin had told him so at one
time or another. But he had *failed*. You could not blame a
man for trying and failing, but he did. If his father had not
failed, his mother would be with him now.

Finn turned back to face his son and sagged wearily
against the wall. The blue eyes that looked at Oisin were
naked—sorrow and anger and shame unguarded.

"Every spring and cave, every mound and standing
stone, anywhere there has ever been the least rumor of
a passage to Tir na nOg, I went there. I went to Tara and
spent long nights on the Mound of Hostages, thinking if
I was taken captive I would at least be through the veil.

I got an audience with the High King's Chief Druid and followed every scrap of advice he could give me."

Finn ran a hand slowly down his face, like a man who has stood vigil through the night. He looked about that tired too, thought Oisin. His father shook his head.

"The way is closed to me, son. I don't know how the Dark Man did it, but he has barred my road. I cannot get in."

"But I can," blurted Oisin. He was surprised at his own words. He did not know where they came from, but he was sure they were true.

Finn gazed at him thoughtfully and then smiled.

"You may be right, lad. You are more of that land than this, after all."

"Then what do I do?" Oisin was strung taught with urgency and crippled with sudden doubt. What *could* he do? He remembered struggling against the invisible door the Dark Man had used to close him into the cave. He had been useless, too weak to pose any threat at all. His thin shoulders slumped.

"You wait patiently, my son." The Finn Oisin knew was back, a man bursting with life and confidence. "You wait, and you hold on to your hope, and you train. I myself will teach you, and all the Fianna, and whatever other teachers you need we will find for you. And when you are a grown man and armed with all the skill and strength and knowledge you can master...then, *then* you will go to your mother's land and conquer the Dark Man and free her."

BY HIS SEVENTH year with Finn, Oisin had already mastered many of the feats of the Fianna. He could outrun the lot of them through the forest without snapping a twig, for he had the speed and grace of his mother's people. In time he would have Finn's strength and height as well, but for now he still had a boy's thin arms and narrow chest.

Not that he was about to admit it. "I am ready now," he insisted. The Fianna were sailing to Alba, and Oisin was determined to join them. "I can fight. Let me come and prove it."

"No, lad. Pass me the oil, so." Finn poured oil into a clay dish, dipped in his fingers, and began carefully oiling every inch of exposed leather on his war-harness. "You can oil my boots, if you are so eager to help."

Oisin's face darkened with anger. His father had dismissed his case without a second's thought, as if he were nothing but a baby. But a baby's tantrum would get him nowhere, so he mastered his temper, stuck out his chest and tried again.

"But why? I am well-trained, by the best, as you said. And I am nearly as tall as you!"

"And half as big around," retorted Finn. With a sigh, he put down his harness and met Oisin's eyes.

"I'm sorry, lad. It's not a joking matter, and your big heart does you credit. And you are right—there is little left to teach you, at least, not until you get your strength. But you must wait for it. If you rush off to battle now, you will be killed. You have it in you to be one of the great heroes of the Fianna, only you must stay alive until you have the might to match your skill."

Oisin scowled. "And what am I supposed to do in the meantime? Stand around counting the days?"

Finn smiled. "I have been thinking on that. And I am thinking that warfare is not your only talent."

Oisin felt his interest quicken in spite of himself. Finn could only be talking about his music. His father seemed proud of how Oisin had picked up some skill on the harp from the bards who stayed sometimes at Almhuin, and clearly enjoyed hearing him sing. But the Fianna were warriors. Oisin had not thought his training could be anything different. Then his father surprised him again.

"I had my own raising with a poet, for some years." Finn laughed at Oisin's look. "I know, you would not think it from looking at me. But I have made some passable poems in my day. And it's how I came to be eating the Salmon of Knowledge, because of my time with him. He thought the fish was destined for himself, but when I was fetching it out of the pan to serve to him, my thumb slipped onto the flesh and got burned, so I popped it into my mouth!" Finn laughed heartily, and Oisin could not help but join in.

"Wasn't he mad, but?"

"I should think. But he was a gracious man, and hid it nicely. 'Ah,' he said. 'Here I misunderstood the prophecy. These seven years I was after thinking the salmon was for me, because of my name, Finnegas, the white. But really, it was for you, Finn, named for your white-blond hair.'"

Finn grew serious. "You have more poetry and song in your smallest toe than I have in my whole body, Oisin. You have come as far as you can in battle skill for now, but it is time you learned your mother's gifts. I am sending you to Cruachan, to study with old Tanai. He took service with me for a time, when he was younger, and he is a man to trust. He will teach you the sweetest music there is to be found in Eire or in Alba. And then you will not only be a Warrior of the Fianna but our Bard as well."

Oisin did not need persuading. He had been entirely focused on becoming one of the Fianna, but now he realized that there was a yearning inside him that could not be satisfied with picking out a few tunes on a harp or singing a marching song.

"When will I go?"

"So eager to leave me, then?"

Oisin shook his head, confused by his own mixed feelings. He *was* eager for something—the learning, the adventure, to test his own wings. But now he saw it would be hard to leave his father, even though Finn himself had been coming and going through his whole childhood.

"It's all right, boy. I am surprised myself at how hard it is to let you go." Finn's big arm wrapped around Oisin and drew him into a hard, quick hug. "We'll make the journey together, once I'm back from this skirmish. And you will keep up your battle practice every day that you are away from us, or I will give each man of the Fianna leave to wallop you into the mud!"

OISIN WAS FORGETTING his mother. At first it upset him, the way she receded from his memory year by year, and he made songs to cement her in his mind and told himself her story in bed at night. But still their time in the cave began to seem like some fantastic dream rather than a memory, and her face faded and dimmed until he could no longer see her at all.

Only her voice remained vivid to him. He could hear it in his own singing even after his voice changed and became deep and resonant.

That was just one of many changes that happened during his five years with Tanai. He had left Almhuin a boy and returned a man, and not just in his broad chest and strong arms. He was steadier in his heart, slower to anger and more sure of his place in the world. The night of his return, after the welcomes and cheering and feasting were done, Finn had walked with him to a lookout point, where they had watched the moon pour silvery light over the bog of Almhuin and talked for long hours. And as the sun was rising, he had held him once more in a father's embrace and said, "Now, if it is still your desire, you are ready to join with the Fianna. You will be my strong right arm, our champion and our voice. Will you take the challenges and become one of us, my son?"

"I will, Father." And Oisin's heart had swelled with the pride of his accomplishment but even more with the knowledge and warmth of belonging.

And as the years went by, the more joy and purpose

Oisin found in his father's world, the more distant his mother's became.

Oisin Remembers

So many of my comrades had adventures in the Land of Youth, but I never went there. There were encounters with its people, to be sure. I will never forget that uncanny night four of us spent in a house full of enchantments. It is all a jumble in my head— the giant prodded down the road by that lovely young girl, the ram that stole our portion of meat, the toothless old man who wrestled the ram and threw it out the door, the sweet water that gave Finn such a colic we thought he was like to die from it. A bunch of Sidhe trickery and malice it was, to my mind, but Finn seemed to take some deep lesson from it all—something about truth and lies and strength—and parted from our host the next day with great declarations of friendship from both sides.

The truth is, I was not looking for a way into Tir na nOg, or to ally with its people. Rather the opposite. I believe now I tried to avoid any path likely to lead there. What had happened to the eager plans I had made as a child? They had faded with my mother's memory.

I knew if I found myself in Tir na nOg, I was bound to find her, to save her or die in the attempt. But so much time had passed. How could she even still be living? And what was the Land of Youth to me? A land of phantasms and cruelty, evil druids and appalling loss. A land of ashes. I had no wish to go there.

Whereas here, in Eire, the ties that held me were strong and clean: my father relied on me, my comrades loved me and I them. I had honor, a growing renown and, one day, the leadership of the Fianna to look forward to. There was no challenge or battle I shied away from in this world. But my mother's world—that world I turned my face from and pretended not to see.

TWENTY-THREE

The once-white strand was blackened and crusted with more hacked and headless bodies than a man could count. How long had they been fighting? It felt like a lifetime ago that the Fianna had made the long march to the strand of Ventry, where the man who dared call himself King of the World had gathered all the enemies of Eire together in one great invasion force. And now it was over. But Oisin could not seem to make his body understand. Every clash of metal and unseen footfall still made him whirl and clutch at his sword.

Oisin looked out over the heaps of silent dead and clouds of shrieking carrion birds, and understood that all of his battles up to now—against the marauding yellow-haired raiders in their long boats, against the chieftains in Alba or Mona who refused to pay their tribute to the

High King—these had all been mere skirmishes and training games.

Not this. This long, exhausting, heartbreaking war at Ventry was the reason the Fianna were given hunting rights and provisioning by the people in every corner of Eire, the reason they were due their rents and honors from the King. For had ever such a massive fighting force landed on these shores, or been beaten back by so few?

But the cost was lamentable. Oisin began to number off the comrades who had fallen: Cael, Fidach, Dubhan, the sons of Baiscne and the son of Cuban of Munster...So many heroes gone, and with them hundreds of their men. In the end the Fianna had triumphed over the best warriors of the world—but there was hardly a man of them left to enjoy the spoils of victory.

The thunder that had rumbled at the edges of the sky all morning at last released a spattering of rain. Oisin squinted through the drizzle, beyond the filth on the beach to the cruel, endless beauty of the ocean beyond. Then he turned his back on all of it and limped off to find his father. The bodies could wait; they'd be none the worse for the rain.

SEVEN MEN AND A handful of dogs made their way silently through the shredding mist of a chill dawn. Loch Lein hid under a silvery blanket, its reedy shores ghostly, but already the first fingers of the sun were probing at the mist, making it rise in thin streamers from its bed and then waft away. All around them, the marshy border of the lake was loud with the voices of water birds waking up and calling to the day.

It had been a long winter, thought Oisin, and they were all glad to be out on the land hunting together. Though his father's new wife had done her best to keep his spirits up, Finn had often been downhearted and brooding in the dark months after the battle of Ventry. But it was hard to be downhearted in the sunrise of a new spring; at least it was for Oisin. He had never lost his childhood love for the wild woodlands, and he remembered now, listening to the invisible chorus in the air, the time Finn had asked them all what music they found best. Conan Maol, a man whose intelligence began and ended with his muscles, had answered, "The sound of playing at games," and Diarmid, predictably, had said he liked best the sound of talk with a woman. But Oisin's reply came to him like a poem, "The music of the woods is best to me: the sound of the wind and of the cuckoo and blackbird, and the sweet silence of the crane."

Which was true enough for this world. But of course there was another music that haunted his dreams: the sound of Sive singing.

Conan, leading the way, came to such an abrupt halt that Caoilte bumped into him. The look on his face soon stilled their protests: slack-jawed and rigid, he was oblivious to dogs and men alike. And then, as if suddenly slapped awake, he pointed dramatically into the silvery mist and breathed, "Is it asleep and dreaming I am, or is the most beautiful woman that ever graced any world coming to us from over the lake?"

Oisin saw her white horse first, its gold trappings catching the rising sun in gleams and glints of light. And then she herself emerged from the swirling mist, and for a long, held breath his heart forgot to beat.

Oisin Remembers

I had thought I knew what beauty was, until Niamh came floating into my sight. She was radiance itself, beyond the words to tell. I remember her cloak was indigo silk with golden stars, as if cut from a clear evening sky, and it drifted down so long it covered her horse as well as herself.

I was pierced with a hopeless longing just to be near her. Surely we all were. It filled me with despair, for how could a perfect creation like her wish to spend any time at all with the likes of us? Yet her eyes—a blue to drown in, those eyes—were not remote or contemptuous. They were filled with invitation— lively, mischievous and gentle all at the one time. And they were looking straight at me.

THE MOMENT HE SAW Niamh's gaze fall on Oisin, Finn knew how it would be. He had always known his son would go back to the Undying Lands, but he had thought it would be in search of Sive. And then the years unrolled, and Finn saw how Oisin's memory of his mother grew dim, and how he did not seek to return but grew ever more rooted in his mortal life, and he began to wonder if his son might stay with him after all.

Not now. He would lose Oisin to this stunning woman, and fair play to him. Finn remembered all too well how it was when he first looked upon Sive. He would have cut off his own foot to stop her tears. And perhaps, after all, this road might lead Oisin to his mother as well. Hope and loss made such a complicated pain in Finn's breast that it took him a while to realize that Niamh had pulled her lovely eyes away from his son's face and was addressing him.

"It is long my journey was, King of the Fianna." Her voice was low and sweet, full of sympathy as if she understood his struggle. "I am Niamh of the Golden Head, daughter of Manannan, the King of the land Underwave."

"What was it brought you to us, Queen?" asked Finn politely, though he already knew.

"It is I have given my love and affection to your own son, Oisin of the strong hands." Niamh cut her eyes to Oisin, who had not once torn away his own, and then resolutely turned back to Finn. There was a right way to go about this sort of thing, thought Finn wryly, and she meant to follow it.

"Though there is many a king's son and high prince gave me his love, I never consented to any of them until I set my love on Oisin."

And just like that, it was done. Oisin shouldered forward and professed his readiness to walk through fire and ocean for her sake, and she gave him a long and pretty speech about the wonders of her land and the joys and honors that awaited him in Tir na nOg, if only he would come and be her husband, but he had no need of her persuasions. He would, Finn thought, have gone with her to live at the bottom of a well.

OISIN WALKED UP TO his father like a man in a dream. He knew well they were not likely to meet again for many years. What words could a man find for such a farewell?

For the first time, he noticed that Finn was aging. Strong and vital still, yes. But age knocked at his door, in the lines around the eyes, the thickness in the waist. The white-blond hair was gray at the temples. Could it be true, he wondered, that he himself would not fade? He had thought only about the joys of living with his love. Now he tried to think about living forever.

Too much. Think now about Finn, and the Fianna, and the love that bound them together.

His father held him in a tight embrace. "Be happy, my son." His voice was husky with emotion. "Remember, you are born to that place. It is your home, as much as this world."

Finn released him, but bade him wait. He fumbled in his kit and then pressed something into Oisin's hands. His craneskin bag. Oisin looked at Finn in surprise. That bag was one of Finn's great treasures. Full of many magical and useful items at high tide, at low tide it would be empty.

"This belonged to Niamh's father, Manannan, long ago," said Finn. "It may please him to have it back. He is a powerful king, a man to have as your ally."

Oisin swallowed, overcome with the enormity of what he was doing, and at the same time in an agony to join Niamh, as if she might vanish away in an instant of inattention.

Finn pulled him to his breast one last time. "Don't worry, lad. Maighneis is a good woman; she'll look after me." He held Oisin then at arm's length, his eyes bright and commanding, and said at last the words that had been in both their minds: "You will seek word of your mother and help her if you are able?"

Oisin stood straight and proud, for one last time a champion of the Fianna. "Upon my oath, I will."

"Your word is the best surety any man could have." Finn nodded, his eyes lingering over his son. "Go now, lad, before your Lady grows tired of waiting."

The horse was slender, but it seemed hardly to feel the weight as Oisin sprang into the saddle behind Niamh. They turned west and flew swift as an arrow toward the sea.

Oisin Remembers

None who know me ever doubted my courage, but if I had been alone on that horse I would have flung myself off before we ever approached Tir na nOg. For when we reached the headland bordering the western sea, the horse waded into the surging foam, gave a loud, ringing neigh, and plunged into the ocean! Yet it seemed he was galloping, not swimming, and we skimmed over the tops of the waves while the strangest sights appeared and passed behind us. I saw sunny palaces and strong fortresses rise out of the foam, hunters and hounds, and once a girl with a golden apple in one hand riding alongside us. And we rode on until the sky darkened and the sea was as if in flames from the sun falling into it, and then we passed through a black storm.

But daybreak brought a calm sea and a bright sky, and then we came to a delightful country, just as Niamh had promised, the trees in full blossom and smooth green plains, and a king's dun that was so much grander than anything I had seen in our world that I had no fitting word to describe it. I saw houses of every color, and palaces of shining stones and crystal, and an army of handsome men and an equal number of lovely young girls coming out to meet us with glad cries.

And Niamh laughed at my amazement, and teased me. "Did I not describe it to you, just so?" she asked. "It was not lies I was spinning but the plain truth. And you will have long life without sickness here with me, and you yourself will be young forever."

THE KING WHO CAME out to greet them was as youthful as Niamh herself, yet she introduced him as her father, Manannan mac Lir.

"A warm welcome to you, Oisin mac Finn," he said. "It is glad I am to receive you here, for your renown and that of your father is well known to our people. And come with me now, that you can be refreshed from your long journey, and we can speak together."

Manannan led them through many beautiful rooms and halls, until they entered a large, bright room with a jewelled throne and many richly carved and cushioned chairs. He motioned Oisin and Niamh to sit, and warm scented water was brought to bathe their hands and faces, and bowls of honey-sweet fruit and tall goblets of cool ale. And while they were drinking away the thirst of their long travels, Niamh told her father that she had set her heart upon Oisin, and that he had come to Tir na nOg to marry her.

The purple plum Manannan was putting to his lips stopped in the air, and he regarded his daughter with, Oisin thought, barely disguised surprise. She held his gaze, and it seemed to Oisin that unspoken words passed between them, for at last the plum continued on its journey, and Manannan nodded at them both as he chewed and swallowed. Finally he favored them both with a broad smile.

"Well, well, it's a wedding feast then that we are planning! You are an honored man, my son, for my daughter has not been one to choose men lightly."

"I am honored, indeed, my lord." If there was ever a time to make a good impression, that time was now, thought Oisin, and he summoned all his eloquence. "For she is my star and my shining one. Were all the women of all worlds gathered before me, it is she alone would hold my heart. And," he added, "as you know of my good name, you will know that I have never broken my word, and that though I am a man angry in warfare, I am gentle in peace. With me she will have kindness, along with my love."

Oisin rose to his feet and pulled the craneskin bag from under his cloak. As he drew it forth, it grew heavy and bulging, filling with its treasures. He walked forward to Manannan's throne, knelt and presented the bag.

"My father charged me to return this to you. It has been in his keeping these many years, and he sends it now with his high esteem."

Manannan reached forward to accept the bag, nodding his thanks. "And all its treasures intact," he murmured, his hands moving over the shapes through the supple leather.

As Oisin returned to his seat, Manannan rose and approached the couple. He took Oisin's right hand and Niamh's left hand in his own in a gesture of blessing.

"You have chosen well, Niamh," he said. "And perhaps not as unexpectedly as I first thought. I will send out the messengers this night, and the celebrations will begin on the morrow."

TWENTY-FOUR

Oisin stretched, luxuriating in the deep softness of the bed and the wash of sunlight stealing into their chamber through the open window. So many windows, and so much sunlight, in this place! In Eire, a window was a rare thing, more trouble than it was worth when it so often had to be shuttered tight against the rain or the cold wind.

Six days into their wedding celebration—or was it seven? Time slipped by so strangely here, it was hard to be sure—Oisin was still seeing new wonders daily. So far, not one could match the woman who slept now in the bed beside him, her golden, tumbled hair kissed by a stray sunbeam. Six passionate nights, six sleepy delicious awakenings, six days spent in the delighted discovery of each other, and still every morning the sight of her, the thought that she was his, filled him with new wonder.

What would happen when the ten days were up, he wondered. It was hard to picture what "normal life" would be to these people. Perhaps he and Niamh would no longer wake up to warm baths and a table laden with fruit, warm bread, quail's eggs and fresh-grilled salmon. But he was more than content to wait out the celebration to find out.

Each evening at the feast there were new guests come to congratulate them, many bringing handsome gifts. More than once Oisin had wished he himself had not arrived empty-handed, with no wealth of his own and no gifts to cement new friendships. At least—thanks to Finn—he had been able to give something valuable to his father-in-law. And then, long into the night, it was music and singing and the telling of tales. He could have listened all night to that music, if not for the even sweeter pleasure that awaited him in their marriage bed.

THE LAST GUESTS HAD taken their leave, all but Niamh's sister Grian and her husband Derg. They had been introduced to Oisin a few days previous, and he had been a little discomfited by the strange, almost hungry way Grian stared at him. She did not seem much like her sister. Though Oisin enjoyed her flirtatious, lively talk, she reminded him of a harp strung too tight. Niamh's calm grace was like a still, deep pool compared to Grian's choppy waters. Yet when Grian had sung two nights ago, all the tightness had disappeared, and she had swept Oisin away in a river of beauty.

Derg seemed a good man, very cordial and warm. He struck Oisin, though, as a man carrying some burden or care: just a hint of strain in his features that stood out in that carefree company.

Now, Niamh had come to her new husband and asked him to join the family in her father's Chamber of Councils. Thinking it must be some final ceremony, Oisin followed, taking his seat with Manannan, Grian, Derg and Niamh.

"The time has come when we must speak of less joyful matters." Manannan, no more the genial host, spoke with the blunt, determined voice of a commander. Oisin, who had seen the same transformation many times in his own father, alerted like a hound on scent.

Manannan continued. "You are a fine young man, and we are all glad that Niamh has chosen you." Oisin shifted in his seat, impatient at the preamble. He had heard more or less this same sentiment for the last ten days.

"But that is not the reason why she came to your land to find you. She was sent by me—by us," Manannan amended, waving his hand to include Grian and Derg.

"For what purpose?" Oisin asked, startled and a little suspicious. All the tales of men being lured and tricked by the Sidhe crowded into his head. Surely his own Niamh would not...

"To ask you to save our daughter, who is Sive, your mother." It was Derg who answered, but Oisin did not notice the annoyed frown that fleeted over Manannan's face at the interruption. He was staring at Derg and Grian, madly trying to recall if he had ever been told anything at all about his mother's family. Derg...hadn't his father mentioned the name Derg? It seemed a common name here, and he hadn't connected the two men.

"My mother is alive?" The words came out more urgent and strained than he intended.

Manannan nodded, regaining control of the meeting. "She is alive, and well enough."

"And under the Dark Man's sway?"

"No. If she were, there would be few left in Tir na nOg free of his chains. No, Far Doirche has been disposed of."

Oisin shook his head, confused. "I don't understand." Something else was nagging at him too, something that had nothing to do with the problem at hand but kept pushing itself forward. He pushed it firmly back. His focus now was on his mother.

Manannan sighed. "It does not sit well on me to admit an error, but in this matter I judged ill. It is possible I allowed my anger at my daughter's consort"—and here Oisin *did* notice Derg flush at the word—"to cloud my thinking. However it was, we left the Dark Man unhindered too long, telling ourselves he was no great threat.

"We were too late to help your mother, and for that I blame myself. It was after she turned against him that Far Doirche became reckless, rage and impatience finally breaking out and bringing his malice into the open. He began a course of random destruction, striking any hapless traveler with his wand and sending him home with instructions to burn down his sidhe, conjuring up curses and plagues and raining them down on one king after another. When that happened, the Old Ones—myself, Bobd, and others—we put our might together against him." Manannan gave a grim, satisfied laugh. "He soon found out his upstart spells were of little use against us."

"But my mother? You said she was all right?" Oisin was more mixed up than ever. If Far Doirche was conquered, what was left for him to do?

"She is not all right!" Grian, her voice strident. "She has not been all right for many long seasons."

Derg leaned forward and touched Oisin's knee. "It was Far's serving boy, Oran, told us what happened, lad. Your mother found a way to defy the Dark Man. He had commanded her to keep her woman's body, but she was able to change just her head into that of a deer, so that she could not sing. You remember she could become a deer?" Oisin nodded, and Derg continued. "When he couldn't make her change back, Far went into a fury and cursed her, so that she would ever be stuck in a deer's form."

He sighed. "With his death, the curse should be lifted. But your mother has not changed. We think she has forgotten how, even forgotten who she is and who we are. She must have some memory of home, for she roams the hills and woodlands near our sidhe, but she will let none approach her, nor does she come near to our dwellings."

And there was the memory he thought he had lost, so present and strong he could taste and hear and smell it.

The sumptuous room faded from his sight and he was back in the cave, pressed against her warm, dappled flank, his head rising and falling with her breath. The fragrant animal heat bloomed like a cloud from her pelt and wrapped him against the cold stone floor and frosty air. His mother. His gentle, courageous, helpless mother. She had seemed helpless on the day Far Doirche dragged her away. And yet she had kept her will and outwitted him. And now she paid the price.

Oisin looked up. Four pairs of eyes were trained on him, waiting. His cheeks were wet with tears, and he took the time to wipe them dry and become once again a man of the Fianna before replying.

"I do not know how I will succeed where you have failed, when you have the same appearance as when she knew you and I am utterly different. But I will try. While there is breath left in my body, I will try."

THAT NIGHT IN THEIR bedchamber, the other thought, the one that had worried at the edges of his mind all evening, pushed its way forward.

"Are you not coming to bed?" Niamh had already slipped under the soft, blue blanket and was sitting against a heap of jewel-colored cushions. Her hair curled in waves around her breasts, a sight to make a man's blood grow hot with desire.

Oisin gazed at her, trying to square the facts in his mind. It was a young woman he was looking at, a lovely girl at the peak of her beauty. And yet it was not...

"Oisin? What is it, love? Is it worry for your mother that weighs on you?" She patted the bed. "Come here and tell me."

He came, and sat, and groped for words. "You are my mother's aunt?" Was he even allowed to marry her, he wondered. There were laws in Eire against the marriage of close blood relatives, but he doubted they covered this situation.

"Yes." She smiled. "Why?" Then her face fell.

"Oisin, you mustn't think…I swear I did not pretend my love to persuade you to come. It was not like that at all. When I found you, you were in that terrible war. And I knew you would not leave your father and comrades in such straits, so I waited and watched, while the killing went on and on. And the more I watched you, the more I came to love you. Oh, my heart, I was in such fear you would die!" Tears glistened in her eyes, making them even more brilliant, and what could he do but kiss her lashes to stop them from falling?

"No, Niamh, no. It is not that. It is much sillier."

"Then what?" She was genuinely perplexed.

"You are as old as my grandmother! I thought you were young!" The words blurted out, sounding as ridiculous as he had feared. But there it was. He was married to a woman who, in his world, would be gray and withered.

She laughed, a merry cascade of music. "Well, not quite as old as her, as a matter of fact. She was well grown when I was born." She laid her hand—a slim, white, young hand—over his. "But, yes, I am nearly her age. *And* I am young, as you will be many years from now. A few seasons, a few sleeps, and we will be much the same age. You will learn—age does not matter for us. Unless you are one of the ancients, like my father, who all believe they are wiser and better than the rest of us."

Oisin shook his head. "It is more than my mortal head can understand," he confessed.

Niamh shot him a sultry look from under her eyelashes and snaked her smooth arms around him. "There is one thing I have learned you understand very well indeed," she whispered. The faint breath in his ear lit a fire that coursed through his veins. He took his wife in his arms— his young, eager, beautiful wife who was, impossibly, some three times his own age—and buried his confusion in the joy of their love.

TWENTY-FIVE

Surely he would never get used to the strange ocean journey to and from Manannan's secret stronghold, however many times he made it. This time the trip was much shorter, landing them on a strand that looked strangely familiar.

But it was not until hours later that Oisin was certain.

"That hill!" He turned on his horse to look backward at Derg, left arm still outthrust and pointing. "That is the Hill of Almhuin!" And they had traveled here from Baile's Strand, but...the road was different. And why could he not see Finn's dun topping the hill?

Derg smiled. "In Eire it is the Hill of Almhuin, home of the mighty Finn mac Cumhail. Here it is simply one of the two hills that keep company with *our* hill." Derg pointed, in his turn, to the first of the approaching hills, and now

Oisin noticed the cluster of buildings crowning its top. "Welcome to Sidhe Ochta Cleitigh."

THEY AGREED THE first thing was for Oisin to see Sive for himself. Accordingly, Derg would fly out at first light to find her and then lead Oisin to the place where she was spotted. After that, Oisin would have to—his mind balked at the word, but what other was there?—hunt her.

He spent a good part of the evening wandering around Derg and Grian's beautiful house and through the grounds of their sidhe. He had never imagined his mother as a young girl or thought of the kind of life she had had. To be accustomed to such luxury and then be cast unprotected into the wilds! How had she ever survived? he wondered.

On their journey he had asked Derg, "Why did you bring me and not my father? Will you not reunite them?"

Derg shook his head. "I do not think so. Not, at least, unless Sive comes back to us and, knowing all that it would entail, insists upon it."

"What do you mean, all that it would entail?"

"Your father has remarried, Oisin. He has a young son, and another child on the way. His Fianna look to him to make them once again a mighty force. Would you have him abandon all these charges to come to Tir na nOg?"

Oisin did not answer. He wasn't sure what his answer was. But Derg was not finished.

"There is another problem. Your father is old."

Oisin's protests were stilled by Derg's raised hand.

"I know, lad. I know he is still strong. He is a great man. But he is more than twenty mortal years older than when Sive loved him, and it shows. What hope is there that she would know him, when she does not even recognize us, who are unchanged? We cannot undo what Time has already done. We cannot make him young again."

And yet they think she will know me? Oisin shook his head and made to ride on, but Derg's next words slowed his pace.

"It is not your appearance we expect her to know. You are the child of her heart, the one who gave her a reason to endure through all the years you were together. You were the source of her strength and her hope, and that hope was that you would survive to manhood.

"We want to show her that her hope came true. Perhaps you will fail, as we have failed. But we think that if anyone can awaken her heart, it is you."

HE STALKED HER patiently, silently, careful of the betraying breeze that might put her to flight. The pain of it—that she would fear him so—caught him unawares.

That was the throbbing of a just-knit wound. When at last he watched her browsing in a glade, and, catching his scent, she raised her head to look at him—that was when the wound's edges were torn apart. For he had thought she would know him. Not in his mind, he didn't. His mind had truly reasoned that she would not. But his heart, he realized now, had believed that when she saw him, she would know him.

She didn't. The startled brown eyes that gazed at him before she bolted away had none of the awareness and intelligence he remembered—oh, *now* he remembered!—from childhood. Those eyes had been his mother's eyes, whatever form or color they took on.

Now they were a wild creature's, nothing more.

THE WOODS WERE nearly dark, and Oisin was most of the way home when the white patches of a magpie's wing flashed in the gloom. Soon Derg was pacing at his side.

"It's slow going through unfamiliar forest in the dark. Thought you could use a guide."

Oisin did not point out that in Eire, there were few places he knew better than the land surrounding Finn's dun. He simply nodded his thanks. He was glad to see Derg. He had had time to think on the long trek back, and what he had concluded was this: so long as he tracked Sive like a hunter, she would respond as prey. He must find a way to gain her trust.

"I need a place that she frequents," he said to Derg now. "Somewhere she goes to rest or drink. Can you follow her as a bird and find one?"

"I already have." Derg's smile was sad. "There is a pool she was fond of as a child. It is where she learned to become one with the wild creatures. Which is, as I gather, what you propose to do?"

"Something like that." Oisin did not have his mother's powers, but he had been a child of the woodland, and he knew how to be still and unnoticed.

"Does she go there often?" he asked.

Derg shook his head. "I can't say. By day, she rarely comes that close to our settlement. The pool is not far into the forest. But I think perhaps it draws her, for I have seen her there several times at dawn. If you were there each daybreak…"

"I will be there each daybreak," said Oisin. And whether she came or not, he would leave food—grains, apples, hazelnuts—for her to find when she did come.

IN THE GRAY HALF-LIGHT of early dawn, a dappled deer picked her way cautiously down the bank. Her dainty prints from several days ago still dented the mud by the pool's edge.

She was almost at the water when she stopped, her wide nostrils flaring. The scent was delicious, fragrant with oats and the sweet heavy odor of fruit. A mound of food lay heaped on a fallen log just off the trail.

The doe stood motionless, torn. It was man-food on that log. She remembered the lean, hungry winters that had driven her, at times, to skirt along the edges of the hunters' fields and orchards, scraping through snow to find fruit or grain heads that had been left behind. There was nothing better than that food, but always it was gained under threat of the spear and the dogs.

She lifted her head, scanning the underbrush around the pool and testing the faint dawn breeze. Yes, there was man-scent about, and—she stretched out her muzzle to an apple that had fallen off the pile and lay near her feet— definitely on the food.

The doe's feet did a comical little dance as the war within—to flee or to eat—played itself out. Then she snatched at the apple, ready to leap away at the least noise or movement as she munched through its sweet flesh. The strange thing was, the man-scent on the food, which should have repelled her, made it all the more enticing.

Sive Remembers

The next morning, the food was there again, and the man-scent was stronger. And though my skin shuddered over my shoulders at the smell of it, I didn't want to flee. I wanted to stay, not just for the grain, but to be near that smell.

When I saw him—a big man with pale hair, on the other side of the pool—his presence was so quiet and still that I didn't bolt but simply retreated into the undergrowth and watched. The food still drew me, yes, but it was more than that. It was like a remembered dream, so many elements that I seemed to have seen before: a deer at the edge of a pool, a quiet person across the water. A big man with yellow hair—why did he feel safe,

*when other men made me run? And his scent—that tantalizing
scent—drew me. Some mornings I had a crazy longing to run
around the pool and bury my nose against him.*

*I never did that, of course. But I did grow accustomed to his
presence. Soon I was coming every morning to the pool, and he
was always there. He spoke to me sometimes in a quiet voice, a
voice that recalled another quiet, gentle voice I had heard once,
and trusted.*

DAYS STRETCHED INTO weeks, and Oisin came to the
reluctant conviction that he had failed to reach his mother.
What he was about, in fact, was taming a deer. That alone
was an improvement; if Sive could be tamed enough to
stay in a stable with the horses, they could, at least, ensure
that she was warm and fed. But she didn't need feeding.
She needed to wake up.

"I suppose Grian has tried singing to her?" he asked
Derg. Derg looked at him in surprise.

"Grian?"

"She must have sung to Sive as a child."

"Of course," said Derg. "And then trained her in the gift.
They spent many hours singing together."

"So," said Oisin. It seemed too obvious to have to
explain. "Music was a big part of her life. I was thinking
it might help her remember."

Derg flashed Oisin a quick, sad smile. "I forget you
haven't known us long. Grian has a voice to make the

heavens weep, true enough, but she has no woodlore whatever. We've never been able to get her close enough for even
a glimpse of Sive."

Derg's eyes grew bright with excitement. His forefinger
pressed into Oisin's chest. "*You* must sing for her, lad."

TWENTY-SIX

"She won't know my voice." Oisin lay in his deep bed staring up at the dark ceiling. He should sleep—he would be rising well before daybreak, to be at the pool before Sive—but he was too jangly with hopes and worries. Derg had found a small harp for him, and soon he would be playing it, and singing, to a half-tamed deer. He told himself that if it didn't work, there was no harm done, that it might take many days, that there were other things to try; but that was not how it felt. It felt like the sudden-death move in a *fidchell* game—everything won or lost in a single play. And what stood to be lost was his mother's life.

"Then she must know the song," Niamh's quiet voice countered. She was curled into him, her breath a gentle rhythm on his chest. Their marriage right now was a far cry from the first ten days, Oisin thought, with him gone every morning, long before Niamh awoke, and buried in the woods half the day. When he had tried to apologize, though, she had given him a round-eyed look of comic confusion.

"And how would I be complaining of that, Oisin mac Finn, when it was I myself searched you out to beg you to do this very thing?" Then she grew serious. "There will be many days for us to spend our time as we please. Now your quest is with Sive, and I am well able to get by in my sister's house without you."

Oisin thought about Niamh's advice. His mother must know many songs from both worlds, but what he needed was a song that would allow her to know *him*. And he knew which song he wanted, only...

"Niamh, do you know any cradle songs?"

"Certain I do. But I haven't the gift, if it's singing to sleep you're wanting."

Oisin shook his head in the dark. "There's a song my mother used to sing to me. I only remember a little bit of it."

Haltingly, he hummed a little phrase of music. "Something about sleep and the moon?" he ventured.

Niamh's laughter tinkled beside him. "Is there a cradle song ever created that doesn't have sleep and the moon in it? But I think I know that tune. Does it go like this?" And she sang him to sleep after all, with a song that had come back to him entire as soon as she began it.

HE FOUND HIS WAY to the pool in the dark and played the harp softly as the night softened into shadowy dawn. He wanted Sive to become accustomed to the sound as she approached, rather than be startled as he began. The tiny instrument had the sweetest, truest voice of any harp he had ever played, and as his fingers grew used to the tight intervals he found first the melody, then the accompaniment to his song.

THE LITTLE DOE STEPPED slowly into the clearing. She paid no attention at all to the food Oisin had left, but kept her attention wholly on him. Her ears swiveled toward the harp, quivering and flicking almost in time with the notes. Was he imagining it, or was she watching him—really looking at him—in a way she hadn't before?

He knew not to stare back, however strong the temptation. He tried to think only about the strings, about the clear notes cascading into melody. He played the harp until the set of her head and haunches told him she was no longer on the verge of flight. It was as relaxed as she was going to be. Oisin drew in a long, slow breath, and he began to sing.

Sive Remembers

From the time he first came to the pool, strange sensations and feelings had been coming to me. I know now they were memories, or fragments of memory, but as a deer all I knew is that many things that should have been strange and alarming seemed instead familiar and safe.

The sound that came from the clearing that morning—it drew me, just the way mortals say the music of my people draws them. I knew that sound. I knew it! Yet I had no understanding of what it was.

And then Oisin began to sing, and all the faint, weak voices that had been whispering to me joined with his voice, and it was like a clear bell sounding in my head, calling me home. And I remembered.

AND THAT QUICKLY, before he was twice through the verses, it happened. She stood before him, trembling and wide-eyed, looking like she might still vanish into the forest if he so much as spoke to her, but without doubt a woman. And he hardly dared look at her, she seemed so frightened, but fought to calm the emotion that shook his own voice. He kept singing. And it came to him, as he sang, how it had once been with them, him just a small boy lying in her lap, Sive stroking back his hair as she sang, and his eyelids growing so heavy he kept forgetting to keep them open.

He kept singing as she stared at her own hands, front and back. Slowly she raised one and felt her head, her face, her lips. She bent forward to look at her feet, and the tears spilled over then and dripped onto her bare toes. At last, hesitantly, she made her way around the pool to where Oisin sat.

It was as if a bird had perched beside him on the log, so light she seemed and so likely to fly. She was weeping almost silently, and Oisin wanted nothing more than to throw the harp aside and sweep her into his arms, but he could tell she was not ready. She had been away so long; he must not rush her returning.

Sive Remembers

The winter I was at Finn's dun, a young boy came in on a bitter afternoon with the tips of his ears and fingers white. His mam scolded him for staying out too long, but he was saucy, saying they didn't hurt, so no harm done.

But once he got inside and sat by the fire awhile, his frozen parts began to thaw. His fingers turned fiery red and the edges of his ears swelled and he cried at the throbbing pain.

That's what it was like for me, as if my heart and mind had been frozen deep in the ice and were now pulled out into the sun and thawing. But the pain of it—all those lost memories and sorrows rushing back—if Oisin hadn't kept singing that little cradle song, I don't know if I would have had the courage to endure it. I held on to that unfurling song and let it pull me in, like a man fallen into the sea hangs on to the rope his comrades throw to him.

The urge to sing was strong in me before I dared try. I could feel the words in my throat, trying to get out.

Moonsilver bless you,
Starshine caress you,
Sleep in the peace of a night free of fear.
Dreams will delight you,
Sunrise will light you,
Slumber till morn, for your mama is near.

But what would come out? I feared I would not know how to form the sounds in my mouth, or that my voice would be a goat bleat or donkey's bray. And—does this sound strange?— I also feared it would be unchanged, for the Dark Man had made me think of it as an evil thing.

But Oisin's song—a baby song, so innocent and uncomplicated—reminded me that before the Dark Man, my song had been my own. I could almost feel my son's little head under my fingers, the curls sweaty from hard play, his forehead and cheeks so smooth and soft.

I began to hum, so softly I could hardly hear myself, but it was there. My voice was true. And then I was singing, singing with my own grown son who I had never thought to lay eyes on again. And the song was like Miach's healing spell. The song was making me whole again.

FOR MOST OF HIS LIFE, Oisin had heard that voice only in his dreams. Now it rose beside him, real as his own, and it was as hard a trial as he had ever faced to keep from faltering.

229

He kept his voice steady as her own grew in strength beside him, doubling the melody he had learned from her own lips. He hung on when her voice rose into a harmony line that brought a new, unguessed-at beauty to the simple song. But then he let down his guard and started really *listening* to Sive's voice, and that's when his own failed him. There was too much contained in that lovely, liquid sound— too much sorrow and fear, too much joy and love, too many memories. He fell silent and then, to his chagrin, was overcome with weeping.

He sobbed into his hands as though he were still six years old, and Sive opened her arms and pulled him against her breast, just as she had when he was little. And then she was weeping too.

It was a very damp day they had, with first one and then the other tearing up at the least thing. They sat together a long time without talking at all, but at last Sive straightened up and took a proper look at her son.

"Look at you, then," she marveled, and was promptly crying again because they were the first words she had spoken in so many long years, and because her joy at seeing how handsome and strong he had become was tempered with the loss of having missed his growing up. And Oisin looked fully at his mother, too, and was shocked at her appearance, for she looked as she had before her last change, half-starved and roughly dressed. She caught him looking with horror at the burn mark on her forearm, and covered it from his sight, saying only, "That's nothing. It was a long time ago." She would not speak, not now, of her time with the Dark Man.

When the sun was high, Oisin rummaged in his pack and brought out food. He broke his round of bread in two and passed one to Sive, who held it, smelled it, and had to dash the tears from her eyes once more. She offered Oisin a shaky, apologetic smile. "You can't imagine how it feels to hold food in my hand."

Eating seemed to give his mother courage.

"Tell me how you fared," she said. "Did...?" The name was like a hurdle in her path. She swallowed, took a run at it and cleared it. "Did the Dark Man send you to your father?"

Oisin nodded. "In a way. We found each other anyway."

Sive released a sigh of relief. "And he raised you well?"

An easy question to answer. "Aye, Mother. He was a good father, and he saw well to my training. I am a champion of the Fianna now, and also their poet and bard." Was. Was a champion of the Fianna, he corrected himself. Did every new gift come with a corresponding loss? Well, there would be time to tell that part later.

"And your father—Finn—he is well?" The question was carefully neutral, but there were deep waters to cross here.

"Yes, he is well." Oisin paused, feeling his way. "Ma, he tried to follow you. He tried and tried, in every way he could think of." The old childhood name came easily and without thought, so intent he was on making her understand this one thing.

"I know. His way was barred." The flat hardness with which she said this made it clear who had done the barring.

It was well into the afternoon before she was ready to ask the question that burdened her the most.

"The Dark Man. Is he...?" She couldn't finish the sentence. Couldn't look at Oisin for fear of the answer.

But he turned to her and very gently tipped up her chin so she could see his head shaking and the truth in his eyes.

"He is dead and gone. Manannan and the others took care of him. He will never be a danger to you, or to anyone else, ever again."

There was more weeping then, and no attempt to stay it, for the dread of Far Doirche had been a weight Sive had carried for more than Oisin's lifetime.

"IT'S NOT LONG 'TIL DARK." The pool, dancing with sun-diamonds at noon, was now murky and opaque from the trees' long shadows. "Will I bring you home now?"

Sive looked at him in alarm, and though her hazel eyes were almond-shaped and filled with her own intelligence, Oisin thought that for a fleeting moment it was a deer's eyes that stared back at him. Then she gave herself a little shake and straightened her back.

"Ah, son. It's a long way back for me still." She nodded resolutely. "Of course we must go home. Only"—and now the eyes were pleading—"they'll be sitting down to evening meal, and..."

"And that's a bit too much to face?" Oisin suggested gently. She nodded gratefully. He could well believe it, imagining Grian's dramatic welcome. He himself was tired to the bone, exhausted as if from a hard day's fighting. He would never have thought talk and tears to be such taxing work.

"Supposing we sneak in the back way, through the cookhouse?" he suggested. "I'll find a servant to run a bath and bring you some dinner—"

"And some decent clothes," Sive interrupted.

"And some decent clothes," Oisin agreed with a smile. It was a good sign, surely, that she was thinking of her appearance.

TWENTY-SEVEN

Despite a generous bribe from Oisin, the serving girl who helped Sive with her bath and dinner did not keep quiet—at least not to the other servants—and so Oran knew of Sive's return before her parents did.

He stayed in the background, though, and not only because it was for Derg and Grian to welcome her first. He was still not quite used to the way people *saw* him now, after all those years of invisibility. It made him uncomfortable to push himself forward, the more so that he was a servant and Sive a lady of the house.

It was Derg who thought to bring them together privately the next morning, the way she would not bump into him in the hallway or serving at table.

Her mouth had gone slack with surprise at the sight of him, and then, laughing and crying, she had rushed across the room and more or less thrown herself into his arms. Oran, beet red and not knowing what to do with his hands, looked at Derg helplessly. Sive's father was smiling broadly.

"She's a wee bit over-emotional right now, lad. Best just to let her be."

"Oran, you're so big!" Sive was feeling his arms and shoulders, completely unembarrassed. Oran blushed an even deeper red.

"You should have seen him eat when he got here," said Derg. "At least, once I persuaded him he was allowed to."

"I was so afraid he had killed you," Sive confessed and burst once more into tears. "I couldn't bring myself to ask, didn't think I could bear to know."

Oran again shot a pleading look to Derg, who made a patting motion with his hand and nodded encouragingly. Gingerly, Oran patted Sive's shoulder.

"Aye, well, he made a good try at it," growled Derg. Manannan's healers had, indeed, brought Oran back from the very brink of death. They hadn't been able to do much about the mangled leg though. That was an older injury, badly healed, that left him with a twisted ankle and a pronounced limp.

"Yet you have him working!" Sive rounded on her father. "After all he did for me, you make him a servant!"

"Sive." Finally finding his voice, Oran interrupted. "I asked him to give me a position. He asked me how he could repay me, and this is what I wanted."

Sive stared at him. "But why? Surely there's no need…"

"There is for me." Oran searched for the words that would help her, a highborn lady, understand. "I wouldn't know how to live like you do. And I don't want to be a burden on Derg, who had no need to take me in at all." He held up a hand, most un-servantlike, to forestall her protests.

"Sive, imagine my life up to now. I have never had a choice. Never earned a wage of my own. Never had companions to work with or friends to pass my leisure with." He gave a short, breathy laugh. "Never had any leisure to pass, for that matter." He spread his hands wide. "This is so much better than anything I've ever known. Perhaps some day I'll want more. But right now, this is what I need."

"You need to learn to be in the world again," Sive said softly. "Just as I do. I should have realized."

Oran nodded. He had had his own exile to endure, even longer than Sive's. He couldn't remember his home before the Dark Man took him.

But he had a home now. He and Sive, they had both been marked by the Dark Man. Yet among his victims, they were the lucky ones. They had come home.

Sive Remembers

I went back to the pool a few days after Oisin brought me home. I needed to look with my true eyes on the place where my life as a deer had begun, and ended. Oisin was a bit alarmed when I told him what I meant to do; I could tell he half-feared I would change again and run off. But I assured him I just needed a little time alone, and he seemed to understand.

The water was dark and still, the woods hushed, and it was easy to imagine it as it had been that first morning, the light just breaking and I a young girl on the verge of her first change. It had been a different doe then, and a tiny fawn, and myself. And who could have foreseen how this one event would color my life?

Shapeshifting had been a gift and a curse to me, as my voice had been both gift and curse. Yet it had protected me from the Dark Man's evil, if not from his wrath. A gift then, but one that came at a high price.

A blackbird's cheery burble broke the silence. I took a final, lingering look around the pool. To see green again! Even in the shadows, the world was rich with color. Never again, I thought, would I trade the colors and faces of my world for the brown and yellow vision of a deer.

Or perhaps, after all, I would. Perhaps a far-off day would come when the memory of my years in exile would be as weightless and untroubling as a wisp of cloud in a blue summer sky, and I could once again play at being a deer. It was possible. After all, in the Land of the Ever-Young, never is a very long time.

A pronunciation guide to the major characters and places in

SHAPESHIFTER

Some names have an extra "half-syllable" tucked into them: a slight *uh* sound, for example, DER-uh-g instead of DERG. I've indicated this with a • symbol. *Kh* is pronounced as a soft *k* in the back of the throat.

PEOPLE

Bodb Dearg (BOVE Der•g) One of the ancients of the Sidhe; Grian's first husband and Daireann's father

Caoilte (KWEEL-tyah) One of the Fianna, and Finn's close companion

Cormac (COR-mac) The High King of Eire (Ireland)

Daireann (DAIR-en) Sive's half-sister

Derg Dianscothach (DER•G Dee-an-SCUH-hakh) Derg of the Quick Speech, Grian's husband and Sive's father

Elatha (EL-a-tha) Sive's first love

Far Doirche (Far DUR•kha) The Dark Druid or Dark Man; evil sorcerer of the Sidhe who pursues Sive. (The more common spelling is *Fear*.)

Fianna (Fee-AH-nah) Elite troop of warriors serving the High King of Ireland

Finn mac Cumhail (FINN moc COO-ul) Leader of the Fianna who protects Sive

Grian (GREE-an) Sive's mother, daughter of the great Manannan

Lugh (LOO) Lugh of the Long Hand; one of the ancients of the Sidhe, related to Finn

Maine and Sarai (MAH-nyah, SAH-rye) Sive's first hosts in Eire

Manannan (MAN-an-awn) One of the ancients of the Sidhe; his realm is the ocean

Murigen (MUR-ee-gan) Woman of the Sidhe associated with lakes; sometimes called a "goddess of lakes"

Niamh (NEE•V) Grian's sister through Manannan; loves Oisin

Oisin (ush-EEN) Finn and Sive's son; his name means "little deer"

Oran (OR-an) Far's servant

Sceolan (Scyo-LAWN) Sceolan and Bram were born to Finn's aunt when she was under a spell that changed her into a hound; they had human wits and were Finn's favorite hounds

Sive (SIVE) Pronounced with a long *I*. I have taken pity on my readers and used the anglicized spelling; the older version is Sadbh!

Tanai (TAH-nee) Bard who teaches Oisin

Tuatha de Danaan (TOO-a-ha day DON-an) Children of Danu; humans call them the "People of the Sidhe." *Sidhe* can refer to either the people or their settlements.

PLACES

Baile's (BOLL-ya's) **Strand**—Beach near present-day Dundalk

Ben Bulben (BEN BUL-ben) Mountain near Sligo

Cruachan (CROO•khan) Royal seat of the king of Connaught, in the modern County Roscommon

Eire (AIR•) Ireland. Used in this book to signify the Ireland of the Celts

Glendalough (GLEN-da-lokh) A valley in the Wicklow Mountains, with two interconnected lakes

Hill of Almhuin (ALL-vin) Finn's fort and headquarters, now known as the Hill of Allen near Kildare Town

Loch Lein (LOKH LEEN) Lake near Killarney

Mound of Hostages—One of the most ancient monuments on the hill of Tara, the Mound of Hostages is said to be a passageway between mortal Earth and the Otherworld.

Mourne (MORN) **Mountains**—Mountain range on the northeast coast of Ireland

Sidhe Ochta Cleitigh (SHEE OKH-ta CLET-ee) Sive's home sidhe

Tara (TA-ra) The Hill of Tara was the political and spiritual centre of ancient Ireland. The monuments on the site are pre-Celtic and are said in legend to have been left by the Tuatha de Danaan.

Tir na nOg (TEER na nog) The land of the Tuatha de
Danann, also known as the Sidhe, which exists as
a (normally) invisible parallel land to Ireland. (Actually it's
more complicated than that, with several seemingly different
"countries" within the Otherworld, but I chose to keep it
simple.) Also referred to as the Land of Youth, the Undying
Lands and the Land of the Ever-Young.

Underwave—Used in this book to refer to Manannan's
kingdom. Manannan is often called the Celtic god of the sea.

Ventry—Now a village on the Dingle peninsula, on the
southwest coast of Ireland.

THE LEGEND OF SIVE

This story was inspired by an episode in the ancient Irish legends of Finn mac Cumhail, famous leader of the Fianna. The original story, or one version of it, goes like this:

Finn was hunting one day, and he and his men were chasing a strange white fawn. The fawn was surprisingly fast, and gradually the men and dogs began falling back, until only Finn and his two wolfhounds, Bran and Sceolan, remained. The dogs finally overran the deer, but to Finn's surprise, when he caught up he found the white fawn resting on the grass, with the dogs gamboling and playing joyfully about her. Finn realized this was no ordinary deer and spoke gently to her. The fawn followed him home, and he commanded she was not to be harmed.

That night a beautiful woman appeared before him. "I am Sive," she said. "I am the deer you spared on the hunt." She was a woman of the Sidhe, and she explained that a dark druid, Far Doirche, had pursued her. He grew angry when she rejected him, and in punishment had laid an enchantment on her and turned her into a deer. (In other versions, as in my story, Sive turns herself into a deer to escape him.) Sive told Finn she had wandered Ireland for three years as a wild deer, until the dark druid's servant took pity on her and told her that she would be safe within the walls of Finn mac Cumhail's dun.

Finn fell instantly in love with Sive, and not only offered her shelter but married her. They were very happy together, but one day the Fianna were called upon to protect Ireland against an invasion, and Finn had to leave Sive behind.

Sive waited anxiously for his return. One day, she saw Finn climbing up the road to Almhuin with his two dogs. Too excited to wait for him, she ran down the road to meet him. Too late she realized it was not Finn coming toward her but the Dark Druid himself, wearing an enchanted disguise. He raised his hazel wand, and the last the servants saw of her, she had been turned into a deer and was being dragged by the neck into the forest. They tried to follow, but Far Doirche's enchantments confused and tricked them, and they stumbled around in the fog after false voices without ever finding their quarry.

Finn was heartbroken on his return and searched everywhere for Sive, but he never saw her again.

However, six years later he and his men were hunting boar on Ben Bulben, when the dogs set up a great hue and cry. The men rushed after them, and Finn was astonished to find Bran and Sceolan set against the other dogs, keeping them away. Behind them sat a little, long-haired, naked boy. And Finn thought there was a look of Sive about his face, and that he might be her son. He took him home and named him Oisin—little deer—and when the boy was less frightened and found his voice, he told them that he had indeed been raised by a deer. They lived in a cave and had everything they needed there. But from time to time, he said, a Dark Man would come. He would speak nicely at first, but Oisin's mother would huddle away in fear, and then the Dark Man would become angry. The last time he came, he drew out his druid rod and struck the deer, and then he led her away. And though she cried pitifully and tried to go back to her son, she was not able but was compelled to follow the man. And though Oisin tried to follow, an invisible barrier held him back. He fell insensible, and when he awoke, he was on the mountain all alone.

That's the last we hear of Sive in the legend. But Oisin's story continues. Years later, when he is a great champion of the Fianna, Niamh does appear to him, profess her love, and take him away to live with her in Tir na nOg. He stays with her for three years and then wishes to return to visit his father and friends. He travels back on Niamh's white horse, only to find that in Ireland three hundred years have passed, and everything has changed. But that's another story!

ACKNOWLEDGMENTS

Thanks go out once again to Richard Marsh of Dublin: storyteller, author, scholar and "legendary tour guide." Over the past few years Richard has generously shared with me research sources, variant versions of legends, theories of the Irish "otherworld" (or worlds?), the pronunciation of Irish names and so much more. Any errors—in pronunciation, geography or mythology—are, of course, mine alone.

I would also like to express my gratitude to the unnamed and unknown people who kept the stories of the ancient Celts alive through many centuries, and to Lady Augusta Gregory, who first pulled them into some kind of logical order and translated them into English, so that those of us who are not Irish scholars can enjoy them.

Last but not least, a special thanks to all the students who attended my workshop during the 2008 White Pine Awards and helped brainstorm solutions to some tricky problems I had encountered with my work-in-progress, *Shapeshifter*. Their enthusiasm and creative ideas were a true inspiration and gave me the final push I needed to finish writing the book.

Holly Bennett is the author of *The Warrior's Daughter* and the Bonemender series. She is the editor-in-chief of *Today's Parent* Special Editions. Born in Montreal, Holly now lives in Peterborough, Ontario, with her family.